SUFFERANCE

GUERNICA WORLD EDITIONS 76

SUFFERANCE

CHARLES PALLISER

GUERNICA
World
EDITIONS

TORONTO—CHICAGO—BUFFALO—LANCASTER (U.K.)
2024

Guernica Editions Founder: Antonio D'Alfonso

Michael Mirolla, general editor
Scott Walker, editor
Cover design: Allen Jomoc, Jr.
Interior design: Jill Ronsley, suneditwrite.com

Guernica Editions Inc.
287 Templemead Drive, Hamilton (ON), Canada L8W 2W4
2250 Military Road, Tonawanda, N.Y. 14150-6000 U.S.A.
www.guernicaeditions.com

Distributors:
Independent Publishers Group (IPG)
600 North Pulaski Road, Chicago IL 60624
University of Toronto Press Distribution (UTP)
5201 Dufferin Street, Toronto (ON), Canada M3H 5T8

First edition.
Printed in Canada.

Legal Deposit—First Quarter
Library of Congress Catalog Card Number: 2023947299
Library and Archives Canada Cataloguing in Publication
Title: Sufferance / Charles Palliser.
Names: Palliser, Charles, 1947- author.
Series: Guernica world editions (Series) ; 76.
Description: Series statement: Guernica world editions ; 76
Identifiers: Canadiana (print) 20230550185 | Canadiana (ebook)
20230550207 | ISBN 9781771838856
(softcover) | ISBN 9781771838863 (EPUB)
Subjects: LCGFT: Novels.
Classification: LCC PR6066.A43 S84 2024 | DDC 823/.914—dc23

For Helen

The girl was not even in my daughter's class—my younger daughter, I mean. The two were the same age—thirteen—and they attended the same school, but they were in different ability groups and had no reason ever to have met each other. Things could so easily have been different, and if it had not been for a trivial remark, she might never have entered our lives. We didn't know her parents. In fact, neither my wife nor I had any idea who her family were for some time after becoming involved with her. The War changed everything. Following the sudden and unexpected invasion, everything closed for two weeks: schools, offices, banks, and many of the shops. During that time all four of us stayed at home listening to the wireless—except when my wife and I took it in turns to venture out, very cautiously, to buy food every few days. The city was a long way from the fighting, and we weren't bombed during the attempt to resist the invasion. But we knew that thousands of our soldiers had been killed or injured or captured and hundreds of civilians had died in the air-raids. It was one of the few times I thanked providence I had no son.

By the second week the streets were dangerous because of the influx into the city of refugees and deserters.

* * *

At the beginning of the third week after the then-capital fell and the government fled abroad, the new regime took control and negotiated an armistice and then a surrender. Things started to return to normal. And yet 'normal' is not the right word since everything was going to be completely different from now on. I returned to work and, as a civil servant employed by the city administration, I saw very clearly how power at the top of the chain of command had passed into new hands even before the occupying forces arrived.

It seemed as if the War was over. That's what we thought. We believed that if our nation had been defeated so quickly and easily, the other countries opposing our Enemy had no chance either. Within a few months, virtually the whole continent would be in the hands of the invaders.

The men who now took control of our city were not people we would have chosen in a free election. (Not that we had had any free elections for some time.) They were the ones who claimed they could defend the interests of the people while working with the occupying forces. The reason they were at first trusted was that they had no record of adherence to an ideology that was now discredited. In effect, it was a kind of malign filtering process: any politician or administrator with decency and scruples fell through the meshes of the net leaving only the self-interested scoundrels. Many of our best people went into hiding for fear of arrest.

When the occupation authority imposed by the Enemy arrived in the third week, these men were in place to greet it. One of the first orders the new authority gave was to require our police to evict from the city anyone who had no right to remain—those whose identity-cards did not show an address inside the urban limits. Within a few days the streets and public spaces had been cleared of the thousands of men, women and children who had been sleeping in the open and begging for food from passers-by. Where they went and what became of them, nobody knew. And nobody asked.

Crucially for what happened to my family, the country was cut into two zones by the occupying power: the Western Zone and the Eastern Zone in which our city lay.

* * *

Now that it was safe, the children started going back to school. And on her first day there my younger daughter came home and while we were having supper, started telling us about a girl she knew very slightly who was in a different class. The girl was living alone in her family's house in a state of high anxiety. Her parents and younger brother had been in the capital when the Enemy attacked. They had been trapped there because all trains had been requisitioned for the movement of troops and the roads were closed to all but military traffic. And when the armistice had brought an end to the fighting and divided the nation in two, the capital—the former capital as I should now call it—was in the Western Zone. They were therefore unable to return or even to communicate since the telephone lines had been cut and the postal service suspended.

Our daughter told us that the poor child was also worried about her elder brother. He had gone into the army when the reserves were called up, and his regiment had been sent to the front as soon as the invasion began. That was all anyone knew at the time.

My wife said: *Surely the child isn't all alone? At her age?*

My daughter said: *There is a servant at the house who is looking after her—the one who brings her to school—but she told me they don't get on.*

I asked: *She has no other relatives?*

My daughter shrugged and said: *Apparently not.*

She told us the girl was very pretty and always very beautifully dressed. Until her parents had gone away, she was brought to school in a big car driven by a uniformed chauffeur. Now she was escorted coming and going by the servant.

She was not liked by most of the other pupils because apart from anything else, she was a show-off and so even the other rich girls shunned her.

I said: *What about the girls from her own community?*

My daughter said: *She's the only one of those at my school who is from a wealthy background since all the others with rich parents go to private schools. Her own kind don't seem to like her either.*

I wondered why the girl was the exception. Why hadn't her parents sent her to a fee-paying school?

Over the next few days my daughter befriended the girl because she had a good heart and saw that despite her boasting, the other child was very lonely. My daughter, too, had not found it easy to make friends—partly I think because of her sensitivity and partly because our social circumstances were modest and she was therefore excluded from the circle of better-off girls whose friendship was most sought after.

* * *

Our daughter talked to us about the girl and told us she had still heard nothing from her parents or her brother. I really don't remember how the idea was first mooted that she should come and have dinner with us. I think my wife suggested it. She was sorry for the girl, and I remember her saying to me afterwards: *If our younger daughter was left alone in this situation, wouldn't we hope that some kind family would take an interest in her?*

So it was agreed that the next day our daughter should invite her to have her evening meal with us on the day following that.

I suppose we realised from the address of the girl's house, and the fact there was a servant living there and the reference to a chauffeur, that her family were well-off; but I have to make it clear we did not take an interest in her because we expected to be rewarded or anything like that.

The girl came to dinner two days later when my daughter accompanied her back from school. She was charming. I thought she seemed much older than our own daughter because she appeared to be so poised—quite the young lady. I remember that as soon as she entered the living-room she crossed to the window and said: *Oh, you have such a lovely view. How I envy you that.*

It's true that there was a spacious prospect over private gardens and a public park and then in the distance you could just see the cathedral. However, the truth must have been that our apartment seemed small and shabby in comparison with what she was used to and so that remark was well-chosen. We were close enough to the railway line to the East for trains to be audible at night. And on this first visit—and now, of course, I see how uncanny it was—she squeezed herself into the corner and said: *Look, you can just see the canal from here. How delightful it looks.*

It was not at all delightful. It was just a bleak industrial waterway. But now as I hear her bright young voice uttering the word 'canal', I find myself shivering.

Then she turned and exclaimed: *Oh, you have a piano!*

She said she was learning the instrument, and so my wife invited her to try ours. The girl insisted our younger daughter play first and then she performed. I am not a pianist myself, but it was clear to me that she was better than either of our daughters in the sense that she executed pieces which were much more technically demanding. It seemed to me—and my wife later confirmed it— that she had been well taught but was not musically gifted, whereas both my daughters had less skill but more musicality. Especially the younger who played beautifully.

I could see that my younger daughter was put out by the girl's superior accomplishment.

Despite the girl's poise there was one moment of awkwardness. She didn't touch the main component of the meal my wife had prepared, and that was in spite of the fact that we had taken account of the dietary restrictions of her community. I suppose she just didn't like it—I forget what it was—or else mistook it for something she was not supposed to eat.

She struck me as a bright, bubbly child. She was pretty and had big green-grey eyes. She smiled and laughed constantly, which surprised me, and it appeared to me that she was completely unconcerned about the fact that the rest of her family were elsewhere and possibly in grave danger. Certainly, you'd think the fate of her brother would be worrying her since he must be a prisoner-of-war if he was not injured or dead.

Our domestic prepared the evening meal on the days she came to us but then left before we sat down to it. On this occasion she had stayed on to help serve it, and the girl couldn't disguise her surprise that we had only one servant and that she didn't live in the apartment but just came during the day.

She talked—in fact, she chattered away—about her life. She appeared to be very unguarded and gossiped freely and openly about her family and her interests. I could see that both my children were dazzled by what she was describing. And what made it more striking was that she did not seem to be boasting. The life she was telling us about was something she took for granted, and it didn't occur to her that my daughters might envy her. At least, that's how it struck me at that point.

She told us about her extensive circle of friends who were the sons and daughters of other wealthy members of her community— their fathers being bankers, lawyers, or doctors. All of them went to school elsewhere—mostly in or around the former capital—and were away now. But when they were back during the holidays they shared a life of visits, outings, music-making, and parties. In the summer there was tennis and swimming at the country-houses they owned or picnics in the woods with chauffeurs in attendance carrying large hampers. Her own family had a villa in the country beside a lake.

I thought how lucky her father was to be able to give his daughter so many advantages. On my salary it was all I could do to treat my children to two weeks by the sea in the summer and a week-end in the capital every autumn to see our relatives.

I kept waiting for her to say that when things had settled down, she would invite at least my younger daughter, if not the elder, to take part in the gatherings, but she did not.

I asked her about her circumstances at that moment, and she confirmed her family's house was unoccupied except for one servant. She wrinkled her nose when she mentioned her and without any prompting told us how much she disliked the woman. She had always been bad-tempered and disobliging, but now that she was in effect *in loco parentis*, she was seizing the opportunity to punish and humiliate the girl to revenge herself against the family that employed her. She catalogued a series of mean-minded decisions the woman had taken. And she believed the woman was dishonest.

At one point my elder daughter was rather tactless and it was the only moment when the girl's poise faltered. When she mentioned that her parents had moved to this country when she was six, my daughter complimented her on her perfect command of our language and then asked her if she was equally fluent in that of the people who live in the Old City. The girl flushed as if she had been slapped and said stiffly: *I don't speak a word of it. It's only for ignorant people.*

My daughter seemed puzzled and said: *But aren't many of those girls at your school?*

She flared up and said: *I have nothing to do with them. They wear the most dreadfully shabby clothes and they don't speak the language of this country properly.*

I might mention here that afterwards my younger daughter told my wife and me something interesting about the child: the girls of her own sort—all of whom were poor since the wealthy ones were at private schools—shunned her as much as she did them, and my daughter thought it was because they resented the way she flourished her wealth by wearing fine clothes and carrying her things in an expensive leather bag from Paris.

To change the subject, I now asked if she had any relatives in the city that she could move in with until her parents returned—aunts and uncles and grandparents—and she explained that because her family had moved to the city only recently, she had no other relatives nearby.

I asked where her parents were staying in the former capital, and she mentioned a hotel whose name I recognised as one of the grandest. It was at that stage, of course, impossible to phone it because the hostilities had severed the phone-lines.

One odd thing. When it came time for her to go, she didn't want to leave. She made some remark about staying the night. Of course there could be no question of that, and my younger daughter and I walked home with her. She lived in the most fashionable part of the city—an area of quiet tree-lined avenues with large detached mansions, many of which were protected by iron gates leading to paved courtyards. She stopped at one of them, and it was only when I saw how big the house was that I realised how very wealthy her family must be. It was a spacious villa on three floors and, as I learned later, it had a large garden behind it with a coach-house at the end.

I asked her what her father did for a living, and it was only now that I found out he owned—or perhaps part-owned because I never got to the bottom of that question—the big department store that was on the corner of the square where the cathedral then stood. The shop sold clothes and household articles, and my wife must have bought things there many times. The name of the store and the girl's family name were not the same, and so we had had no reason to connect them until she revealed the link.

The servant opened the door, and she didn't look like a pleasant woman. She was about fifty, with a hard, thin face that seemed to be fixed in a permanent scowl. She glared at my daughter and me and didn't soften her gaze when she turned to the girl. She just said: *Hurry along now, miss. It's later than you promised.*

The girl behaved very sweetly when we said goodbye. She kissed my younger daughter and shook hands with me and said: *You've been so kind. Really, so very kind.*

It was such a strangely grown-up remark. She must have heard her mother say it. Or even perhaps picked it up at the cinema from some romantic foreign film. Then she suddenly stood on tiptoe and kissed my cheek and whispered: *I wish you were my daddy.* She turned and hurried into the house as if she dared not stay a moment longer or she might break down in tears.

That was the remark which triggered everything that followed. In that moment I felt for her as if she were my own child, and the idea came to me that was to have such far-reaching consequences.

As my younger daughter and I walked home, I discovered to my surprise that she had decided she did not like the girl after all—even though it was she who had first taken an interest in her. She called her false and contriving and snobbish. She had exuded superiority: our piano-playing was inferior; our apartment was cramped; and our best food wasn't good enough for her. I said she had behaved impeccably given that she was in a milieu she could not have been used to. Of course there were things about the way we lived—and even the way we spoke—that must have surprised and perhaps offended her, but she had taken care not to let it appear. Would my daughter have preferred her to have spat out the food? Surely it was better just to have left it uneaten. She was not persuaded. She accused her of showing off with all her talk of her friends and their affluent lives, but later I wondered if the fact that she wasn't—apparently—boasting when she talked of those things but just taking them for granted as perfectly normal, might have been what had irritated my daughter, who was generally very sweet-natured.

When we got home, we found that my wife and elder child had been as impressed by the girl as I had been.

My elder daughter rhapsodised about her appearance and said: *Her clothes were exquisite. You can say what you like, but at least those people know how to dress.*

Her sister said: *She only dresses well because she's rich.*

My elder daughter said: *It's not a question of money but taste. You should learn from her. You take no interest in your appearance.*

Of course that annoyed her sister and the two of them had quite a spat about it. Seeing them bicker I could not help wondering whether my younger daughter—or even my elder—would have been capable of conducting herself with the girl's aplomb and assurance if she had had to spend an evening with complete strangers from a level of society very different from her own.

The gap in age between my daughters—three and a half years—was an awkward one. It meant they shared very few interests, and the elder child felt a little threatened by the younger who was clever and gifted and good at things that her sister was not—academic work and music. On the other hand, she was less adept socially and less interested in clothes and fashion and make-up. The younger girl's academic ability was all the more reason why she did not feel that her sister had any right to lord it over her. They squabbled frequently.

Poor little chit, my wife said later when we talked about our guest. *Just think what she must be going through. Not knowing what has happened to the rest of her family.*

I could see that those words had had an effect on my younger daughter, and she made no further criticism of the girl that evening.

That night when my wife and I were alone after the girls had gone to bed, I raised with her an idea I had been turning over in my mind. I said: *Why don't we invite the girl to come and stay with us until her parents get back?*

She was against it and thought we shouldn't get involved since we had no relationship with the family. I said: *It would only be for a few days. The situation is returning to normal, and her parents will be able to return to the Eastern Zone very soon.*

She looked dubious and said: *There's something about the girl—despite the charm and the cheerfulness—that bothered me.*

I asked: *Do you mean she is pretending to be something she is not? That she is concealing a malign personality?*

My wife said: *No, I don't mean that. She's too young for such deliberate deception. I don't believe there is anything bad in her. Not exactly. But I think she is troubled and she could create problems for us if we have her to stay.*

I repeated that it would only be for a short time. A couple of weeks at the most.

She said: *It's an open-ended commitment, though. We don't know how long it would be for.*

Then I used as an argument something that had been in the back of my mind since I had discovered who the girl's father was. I told her how much our lives would be improved if I were able to find a better-paid post outside the municipal council—especially given the upheavals it was going through with the new occupation authority making radical changes and dismissing many of the staff in order to replace them with its friends. My position in the Department of Finance was not secure since I had no political connections with the new people in power. My hope was that the generosity we extended towards the girl would be balanced by her father's towards me. In short, he might offer me employment in his company since such a business needs people capable of doing the work of an accountant.

My wife saw the point and after a little more discussion, she consented to my proposal.

I would not have gone ahead if she had not agreed. I never let myself forget what she and I had been through in the past, but I believed all her difficulties were safely behind us. The last thing I wanted was to provoke a recurrence of her illness.

* * *

At breakfast the next morning we told the girls what we had decided. To my surprise, my younger child jumped up red in the face and said: *I don't want her here!*

The elder girl said: *I think it's an excellent idea.* She turned to her sister: *You could benefit a great deal from her presence. She'd improve your piano-playing and also your manners.*

It was good-hearted and mature of her to suggest that, though she expressed it rather tactlessly.

The younger said: *It's not fair. She has a beautiful house to live in with a servant to look after her. Why does she need to come to us? If we wanted to be with her, couldn't we move in with her? She's told me her house has got six bedrooms. We've only got three.*

Then my elder daughter asked: *Where would she sleep?*

My wife said she and her sister would have to swap rooms because the younger's room had only a single bed and was small, whereas she slept in a double bed which would accommodate the two girls. My elder daughter took that badly and now supported her sister in opposition to our proposal. She argued it would be unkind to take the girl away from the things she was used to: the house, the food, the customs, and so on.

Now my wife deployed the arguments I had used to win her over: the girl was too young to be left to a servant who was unkind to her; there was no saying what the woman might do or fail to do.

My younger girl softened towards the proposal and agreed it would be fun to have a friend of her own age in the apartment.

Her sister continued to resist and said: *Why don't some of her own people take her in?*

I said: *Remember that her family have not been settled long in this city and have no relatives here.*

She said: *Surely they have friends? We heard enough about them last night.*

I said: *Apparently none are in a position to help.*

Thinking about it later, it did seem odd that her parents had not arranged for friends to keep an eye on her. But I assumed they had expected to be away for only a few days.

My elder daughter went on objecting, but my wife and I had made our decision. We gave our younger child a letter to give to the girl at school that day inviting her to be our guest until her parents got back. She was to come to us that very day if she wished, and I said I would meet her and my daughter after school at her parents' house where I would explain the situation to the servant and collect what possessions the girl needed to bring.

Once they had accepted that it was going to happen, the two girls set about cleaning the apartment, exchanging bedrooms, and tidying up their things to make room for a third girl in the brief time they had.

* * *

So that afternoon I left my office a little early and waited outside the girl's house until she and my younger daughter arrived from the school escorted by the servant. I could see that my daughter was sulking. We went into the house, and when we were out of the servant's hearing the girl told me how grateful she was for the invitation. Then in a lower voice she begged me not to tell the woman anything about who I was and where I lived. I was surprised and objected that I had no choice but to do so. She looked worried.

While the girls were upstairs packing I told the servant that, with her consent, the girl would move to our apartment. I could not tell if she was pleased or annoyed—pleased to be rid of her charge or annoyed at not having the opportunity to lord it over her. To my relief she raised no objection because it would have been difficult to decide whether she could have over-ruled the idea. I had made the point about her permission being required merely to mollify her. If she had refused to grant it I don't know what I would have done. I suppose I would have had to bow to her decision.

She said rather meaningfully: *Well sir, I wish you the best of luck with young madam.*

I told her my surname, which is a very common one, and she appeared to have misheard it because when she repeated it, I realised she had mistaken it for a similar and also very common name. Instinctively I did not correct her. Thinking about that later, I realised I felt a vague disquiet about telling her much about myself because of what the girl had said about her malice.

She asked for my address, and I told her the name of the street and said that everyone there knew which was the building I lived in. That wasn't quite true since it was a long street of apartment buildings rather than a short one with a few houses on it like the wealthy one we were in—which is what I suppose I was implying.

I went upstairs to see why the children were taking so long. I found them in the girl's bedroom where they were looking at an object on a dressing-table that I could not identify. It was an elegantly made small wooden cabinet with tiny drawers and a mirror above it. It was inlaid with woods of different colours and was obviously an expensive artefact. At the base was a carousel with little pots painted in bright colours sitting in their silver nests.

My daughter was saying: *It's adorable. How I'd love to have one of those. Do you want to bring it?*

The girl screwed up her face and then said: *You take it. I don't want it.*

My daughter was embarrassed and protested she had not meant that, but the girl was insistent. I could see the servant who had followed us upstairs looking on dourly.

I asked what the object was and learned that it was a 'vanity carousel' for putting on makeup. It was designed for a second person—a maid or one's mother—to assist the young female being made up. I pulled open the drawers and found they contained powders and scissors and tweezers and implements for manicure and pedicure.

The girl said: *Mother and I never use it.*

I thought it was highly unsuitable for a child of their age, but my daughter begged me to say yes and eventually I agreed that we could take it with us. I carried it down the stairs and the girls came after me, my daughter bearing an armful of clothes and the girl holding a box made of cherrywood about the size of a large briefcase. They packed everything into a suitcase and when they were ready to set off, the girl was still clutching the box which she said held the objects she could not be separated from.

Because of the suitcase, I hailed a taxi to take us home. Seeing our neighbourhood through the girl's eyes a few minutes later, I felt the contrast between it and the district we had just come from. I explained to her that my wife's grandfather had built and owned the whole building at a period when the area was much more fashionable than it later became. We had inherited the apartment that he had designed for himself, and we had stayed there, even while the district grew shabby, from a sentimental attachment to it. It was on the top storey and unlike the others, occupied the whole floor and was therefore twice their size.

She wasn't very interested, and I didn't explain that my wife's father had had to sell the rest of the apartments or that we were regarded by some of our neighbours as 'superior' and were resented and accused of 'putting on airs'.

It was true that I was the only person on the stair who had a professional position, and my salary was higher than that of the others and we were the only people in the building who employed a domestic—though only part-time. The other tenants were skilled artisans: a clockmaker, a tailor, a joiner, and so on.

The concierge had the ground-floor apartment by the streetdoor and oversaw it through a grille a few steps inside the building. She was an inquisitive and somewhat servile widow whose son lived with her—a surly lout in his early twenties who had no trade but helped on building-sites or workshops and was usually out of work and often drunk on money given him by his mother.

I should describe our apartment since its layout will be crucial in what comes later. It had a large kitchen, a very big living-room which we also used as a dining-room, and a small study in which I did my paperwork and sometimes, to be honest, just hid from the all-female environment. There were also a bathroom, a lavatory, a tiny scullery off the kitchen, and a small utility room for storing things. And, as I've mentioned, it had three bedrooms.

By the time we got home that evening my elder daughter had moved her things into the smallest bedroom and the two younger girls now installed themselves in what had been her room.

My wife and I were summoned to see the ceremonial opening of the cherrywood box. It was a handsome object that was bright red and varnished and had gleaming brass handles and hinges. The girl placed the box on a table and unlocked it with a key she wore round her neck. She showed us what she called 'my most treasured possessions' which consisted of some semi-precious gems as well as some fine paste jewellery. One item was obviously valuable: a necklace of coral pearl-drops strung on a silver chain. I could see how excited my younger daughter was and wished I could have given her such valuable presents.

The girl made a gift of a bracelet of rhinestones to my daughter and told her she could have the use of the coral necklace for as long as they were sharing the room. She then brought out an object wrapped in layer upon layer of tissue paper, and it was eventually revealed to be an antique oriental doll that had a beautifully painted china face and was dressed in exquisite silk and brocade. Her father had been given it by a business associate and had passed it on to her when she was nine, but because it was so precious, she was not allowed to play with it. (My wife thought it dated from the late eighteenth or early nineteenth century and was certainly good enough to be in a museum.) Now she was too old to play with dolls, but she had become fond of it. Having taken those things out, she locked the box.

To my relief the two younger girls were now getting on well. It became apparent that evening, however, that my elder daughter had taken umbrage at not receiving a gift herself despite having sacrificed her room. My wife and I had often talked about the fact that she was always on the watch to see if her sister were benefitting from some favour which was withheld from her, and we thought that was because it must have been hard for her to lose the status of only child when the younger girl was born—though we had made a great effort to reassure her that she was as loved as before. We showed no favouritism towards either child.

It was one of my bitterest regrets that my two daughters did not get on better. The younger had a sweet, open nature and again and again tried to soften the heart of her sister, who from her birth had resented her existence and had come to believe that the arrival of her sibling had brought about their mother's alienation from herself. She had been too young to understand what was really happening to her mother at that period.

* * *

At supper the girl talked again at length about her family's villa in the country and what fun she and her friends would have there when her parents returned. I think we were all waiting for her to include my daughters—at least the younger—in the anticipated jollification, but she said nothing about that.

All of that only served to make my elder daughter more hostile towards her, and later that night when the younger children had gone to bed, she raised the subject with my wife and myself and accused the girl of being a toady and insincere and boastful.

My wife said: *She says those things because she wants to be accepted. It's not really boasting. It's a plea to be liked.*

My daughter was not mollified.

Thinking about the beautiful things I had seen at the girl's house—the pictures, ornaments, silverware, carpets, and so on—I wondered if the house and its contents were safe in the custody of the servant. If she were not completely honest—as the girl had suggested—it would be tempting and very easy for her to steal some of the smaller items. It occurred to me now for the first time that the girl's father would not be pleased if the result of my removing his daughter from the property turned out to be that it was pillaged and ransacked.

* * *

Because I wanted to avoid paperwork and questions from the school, I decided there was no necessity for anyone there to be told that the girl was lodging with us. And so the next morning before the two younger girls went off to school together on the tram, I told them not to mention the new arrangement to anyone.

That evening I was working on some papers in my study after dinner when there was a tap on the door. The girl came in with a charming smile and asked if she might have a word with me. I invited her to sit down. She told me she had come because today was Friday and at home her father gave her the weekly allowance due to her every Friday evening after dinner. She had not, of course, received any cash since her parents had left for the capital. With a delightful smile she asked me if I could 'advance her a sum on account', which must have been a phrase she had heard her father use. I said I was perfectly happy to do so and that I gave my daughters such an allowance each week—also on Friday evenings so they could indulge in a few treats over the week-end. I named the figure that I gave my younger daughter and said she would receive the same amount. She looked surprised and—really in the most winning manner—said her father always gave her such and such a sum. I was astonished. It was three times what I gave my younger child and much more than I gave even the elder. (I worked out later that it was two-point-five percent of my salary after tax.)

However, with the reflection that her father would reimburse me when he returned, I gave it to her on the strict understanding that she should not tell either of my daughters about it. I had to tell my wife, of course.

I have to be completely frank in everything or there is no point in my writing this. At that stage I found in the girl qualities I wished my daughters possessed. She was vivacious, generous in spirit, charming, mercurial, and, perhaps above all, deeply affectionate and demonstrative. There was an openness to life, a capacity for love, that made her very attractive. I won't say those qualities counted for more than my daughters' good points, but both my wife and I had been raised in families that were disciplined, hard-working, and undemonstrative, and we had brought up our daughters to be obedient, quiet, and reticent. I suppose that had been at the cost of a degree of spontaneity.

To my regret, I wasn't entirely frank with my wife at that time. I told her I regarded the money I was giving the girl as an investment and I was keeping a detailed schedule of my expenses on her behalf. Her father, I hoped, would be so grateful that he would reward me with a well-paid post. My wife didn't quite believe me, and she was right not to. The truth was, as I grasped only much later, I loved to see the gratitude and excitement that blazed in the girl's face when I handed her the money. The way she hugged herself and blurted out what she intended to buy with the cash.

I owe it to myself to make it plain that I loved my daughters—the younger especially—and that I never felt as warmly towards the girl as I did towards my own children; yet I found myself at that point wishing more than once that they had some of her vivacity and unguardedness.

* * *

The next day, Saturday, we all took the tram into the city centre after lunch. While the other four went to the cinema, I headed for the main office of the telephone company by the cathedral because I had heard that the phone-lines between the newly-imposed zones had just been restored. It was a long and tedious process. Because there was now a border, I had to fill in a form giving my details and the purpose of the call, and have it stamped by an unseen bureaucrat.

When I got through to the hotel in the capital on a very poor line, I learned nothing. The person I spoke to seemed to be an idiot who claimed never to have heard the name of the girl's parents.

That evening I wrote and posted a letter to them at the hotel explaining that my wife and I had taken in their daughter. I assumed it would reach them.

* * *

The following week passed without incident. By the end of it, two things had become apparent. One was that the parents of the girl had not responded. Another was that the girl was unable to be alone or to amuse herself with a book or by listening to the wireless as both my daughters did. She had to be with people and had to be talking. Moreover, she had a compelling need to be the centre of attention and would pester others in order to be noticed if she felt ignored. She chattered the whole time about her friends and the fun they all had doing various glamorous and exciting things.

When she spoke of such matters my younger daughter was entranced—envious but fascinated. My elder daughter, however, was getting more and resentful of the 'interloper' as she called the girl when she wasn't present. I often saw her watching her little sister when she was staring round-eyed at the tales of balls and evening-gowns from Paris and dances at grand hotels issuing from the girl's mouth. She was envious of the girl for stealing her sister's admiration and respect and perhaps even her affection, and that was surprising because she had always treated her younger sibling without much obvious warmth.

On one occasion when the girl was out shopping with my wife, my elder daughter called her 'a spoiled little princess'. My younger daughter defended her new friend and accused her sister of being nasty to the girl because she was jealous that her little sister had a friend who was so much more sophisticated than anyone she herself knew—and also wealthier. That enraged her—probably because it was close to the truth. After that she would often accuse the girl of snobbery, materialism, and showing off. Those rows, of course, took place only in the girl's brief absences from the room or from the apartment.

It was about this time that the occupation authority rounded up all the troublemakers who were powerful in the trade-unions and had caused strikes before the invasion. Very few of us shed tears on their behalf.

* * *

I was forbearing towards my elder child because I knew she had been more seriously affected by political developments than the younger who, still at school, had not really felt much difference as a result of the Occupation. I knew well how she felt when she failed her exams. I had experienced that myself, after all. It was the more bitter for her because there was no external reason, as there had been in my case, and the truth was simply that she was much less 'clever'—whatever that means—than her sister. She knew it and resented it. I could see how she tried to justify to herself her poor performance by saying that I had not helped her because I had been preoccupied with her mother's health.

Though not academically gifted, she had considerable artistic talent. Her great ambition was to study couture and become a dress-designer, and she had intended to start in the autumn at the College of Fashion in the former capital. It wasn't quite what I had hoped for her, but I was perfectly resigned to it. The division of the country into two zones in different nations had now made that impossible, and while the course of study offered by the city's own College of Art and Design would have been a poor second-best, that alternative was also barred to her because the College had so far been unable to re-open because of the invasion and then the Occupation. She was therefore in an uneasy limbo waiting to see if even that inferior option would be available.

Her unhappiness was making the atmosphere in the apartment more difficult and was, I thought, the reason why she was so negative towards the girl. Then I had an idea. I remembered she had been hurt that her sister had received such a handsome present from the girl as the vanity carousel, and it occurred to me that I could improve relations by buying a gift and asking the girl to present it to her as if it were from herself. I talked it over with my wife, and to my surprise she advised me against it because she thought any kind of deception—even for the best of motives—created difficulties. I therefore dropped the idea.

Meanwhile, the border between the Eastern and Western Zones showed no sign of being opened. In fact, the Enemy appeared to be preparing to incorporate the Western Zone into its own territory and frequent references were made by its wireless stations and newspapers to its historical claim on that part of our country. It therefore seemed less and less likely that the girl's parents would be able to return soon.

The girl took no interest in the news on the wireless or in the newspapers, as though it had no bearing on the circumstances of her family. But at the same time, she kept asking to go back to the house to find out if her parents had returned, and it was as if she could not connect the great events in the outer world with what was happening in her immediate circle. Without quite knowing why, I did not want her to visit the house every few days, and so I said the servant there knew how to contact me if there was any news. (That wasn't quite true, as I've mentioned, since she had got my name wrong and knew only the name of the street I lived in.) And I explained to her that since no civilians had been allowed to cross the border, her parents and younger brother must still be in the Western Zone. I said I would call at the house at least once a week to see if there were any message from the rest of her family.

I didn't think the small deception mattered since I was determined to keep my word and visit the girl's house frequently.

Because she was expecting to hear from her parents, the girl rushed to the door of our apartment whenever anyone knocked. I found it irritating, and it was also awkward having to explain to our callers that she was a schoolfriend of our daughter who was just visiting that afternoon or that evening, because we had decided to mention to nobody that we had taken the girl in.

On the Wednesday evening of that week the girl and I went into the room the girls shared to look for my wife and found her helping our younger daughter to make herself up using the vanity carousel. I wasn't quite sure I was happy about encouraging that sort of narcissism. But when I raised those doubts with my wife later that evening, she said: *It's perfectly normal at that age for a girl to begin thinking about her own attractiveness. I'm glad she's starting to.*

One thing I didn't mention to her was that when we had entered the bedroom I had been struck by the expression on the girl's face as she watched my wife showing our daughter how to apply makeup before they had realised we were there. I can best describe it as 'a thoughtful frown'.

A little later I heard her say: *Your mother's really nice to help you with that.*

* * *

That Friday evening I gave the girl her pocket-money as before. The fact that she had so much more cash to spend than the other girls had already been noticed by them and was causing friction—and that was even without their realising I was giving it to her. They assumed she had brought it with her. Yet she was generous with the money, and when the younger two went out together she would buy my daughter little gifts of chocolate and costume-jewellery. She paid for cinema tickets for both of them twice that week when they went to a film she was anxious to see but my younger daughter less so.

For the girl, being able to gratify a passing whim and to bestow gifts was more important than the objects or the experiences that she purchased. My daughters, brought up to be thrifty as they had to be, placed more emphasis on the value of the purchase.

I began to understand why the girl had not made friends at school. I could imagine how her ostentatiousness annoyed her fellow-pupils and made her disliked. Her wastefulness—her impulsive purchase of something that she quickly tired of—annoyed me. She had everything she wanted in comparison with my daughters who had had almost nothing.

Her obsession with her appearance was striking. (In that respect she was more like my elder than my younger daughter, who was happier with her nose in a book than almost anything else.) She spent hours making herself up and trying on different combinations of clothes and would come bouncing into the living room and twirl round and round in front of the rest of us like a professional mannequin. My elder daughter, despite her reservations about her, could not resist this appeal to her professional expertise, and the only times when the two girls got on well together were when they were discussing matters of fashion and trying on clothes or talking about make-up and hair. They would sit together leafing through illustrated magazines depicting the latest Parisian couture or fashionable hairstyles or expensive jewellery.

The passion that my younger child and the girl shared was the cinema, and for as long as it was permitted, they went together once or twice a week. In the evening they would pore over magazines and read each other stories about their favourite film stars.

I noticed how rarely the girl spoke about her parents—particularly her mother. She once remarked: *Mummy says she has no respect for people who want quality but aren't prepared to pay the price.*

I felt that was a strike at thrift and so I said: *Isn't the ability to find a bargain admirable?*

She said: *That's what Daddy says. But Mummy says that's a vulgar attitude. You shouldn't haggle over something you really want.*

When I complained to my wife about the girl's vanity and boastfulness, she never responded, and I had the impression that, though always on the watch to defend her daughters, she had more sympathy for the girl in regard to these matters than I had.

* * *

The next day—Saturday—things came to a head. All three girls went out shopping in the afternoon, and the first I knew of trouble was when my younger daughter came to me in tears after they had got back. Through her sobs I was able to make out that the girls had quarrelled. My daughters had asked the girl how it was that she had so much cash all the time, and she had revealed—heaven alone knows why!—that I was giving it to her.

I was furious with her for that. I could only assume her motive was to make trouble.

I took my daughters into the study and explained that my giving so much more cash to the girl was a financial transaction between myself and her father. It was a loan to him that would be repaid—along with various other expenses incurred on the girl's behalf. Because they were not mollified by that, I went on to say it was in our interest as a family to treat the girl well because of the possibility—and I stressed it was no more than that—that her father might reward me for our kindness to her by offering me a better-paid post in his firm.

I felt I had to tell them that to make them realise I had not shown favouritism to the girl. At the same time, I impressed upon them the importance of not talking about that to her because I did not want her to think I was being kind to her only because I expected a reward from her father. Finally, I promised that from now on I would give her only what I gave my younger child. That satisfied my elder daughter, but the younger pleaded that instead, I should raise both their allowances to the figure I had been giving the girl. That was impossible and I made it quite clear.

Then I talked to the girl on her own and told her my decision. She took it very badly. Her lower lip began to wobble and she said something about liking all of us so much and she had thought we liked her in return. I couldn't see the relevance of what she was saying and assured her it had nothing to do with whether we liked her or not. Of course we liked her. We were all very fond of her. But I could not afford to give her such a large sum and it was, besides, unfair to give her so much more than my own children.

* * *

The next Monday after work I made a slight diversion and went into the department store associated with the girl's father. It seemed to be functioning as well as usual—apart from the privations that everyone was enduring like the lack of heating and the shortage of certain items which left the shelves looking somewhat bare. Clearly someone was running the business. Was that a partner or just a very competent manager? If the latter, was he cheating his employer? Because of my training in accountancy, I could imagine how easily that could be done and I longed for the opportunity to inspect the accounts.

I might as well mention here that from now on I made it my practice to drop in on the store every few days to see how it was running. And on days when I didn't do that, I often took a round-about route that, with a change of trams, allowed me to walk past the girl's house. There was no discernible alteration in its appearance. Once a week, usually on a Tuesday, I rang the bell and went in for a brief conversation with the servant. The first time I did so she was very guarded and we just talked in the hall long enough to establish she had heard nothing from any of the family.

She showed little curiosity about the girl and no desire to have her return. I couldn't help wondering if that was because she was helping herself to things from the house.

* * *

During the remainder of the third week after the girl's arrival things deteriorated between the three youngsters. Far from clearing the air, the events of Saturday evening when the issue of pocket-money had been brought up seemed to have made the situation worse. From that point onwards it seemed to me that the girl set out to make trouble between the sisters—never far away at the best of times.

That Wednesday the girl spoke at supper about the pastimes and entertainments she had enjoyed with her family and friends. I had thought on the first occasions when she had described her opulent life that she was not consciously showing off when she talked of the luxury in which she and her circle lived, but now I began to see I had underestimated her. She was trying to irritate my elder daughter and knew precisely how to rub in the fact that she had enjoyed so many advantages that my daughters had not. The more captivated my younger child was by these stories, the more annoyed the elder became both at the boasting and at the naïve enchantment of her sister.

* * *

Two days after that, my younger daughter came to her mother and me in tears after school to say the girl had just told her she could have the use of the vanity carousel only for as long as they were sharing the room. My daughter was upset because she was convinced it had been an outright gift. We told her it must have been a misunderstanding and that it was right and proper that such an expensive article—and a gift from her parents—should be returned to the house when the girl went home.

Things became more and more difficult from that point onwards. The oriental doll became a source of irritation. The girl was so fond of it that she carried it backwards and forwards between the living-room and the bedroom. She talked to it and held long conversations with it—often in whispers. Sometimes she seemed to be complaining to the doll about one or more of us. It was distracting and it particularly irritated my elder daughter.

The girl was annoying all of us in one way or another and creating friction between us. My wife was upset by the fact that she had revealed herself to be very finicky about food, refusing to eat many of the things my wife and the domestic prepared, even though they observed the dietary restrictions she had explained in great detail to my wife. The problem was essentially that she was used to delicate and expensive food of a kind that we could never have afforded and that, with the War and the Occupation, was virtually unobtainable anyway.

More seriously, she would hog the piano when one of the other girls wanted to play and only give it up very reluctantly. Worst of all, she often refused to do what either of us told her and then answered back. We could not let her get away with that sort of behaviour because of the precedent it would create for our daughters. And so we had to reprimand and even punish her more and more often.

I realised the girl had a mere veneer of charm which was being rubbed off by familiarity. And I began to feel a certain annoyance that she showed no gratitude to my wife or myself for the inconvenience and even perhaps the risks we had incurred on her behalf. I found it impossible to close my eyes to the element of slyness in her character. She was charming when it suited her interests and used that ability to manipulate others in a manner said to be characteristic of her race. At first she had been well-mannered and respectful towards my wife and myself, but now that that approach was not working she gradually started being rude and offhand. It seemed unfair that a child who had had so much lavished upon her should have developed so much worse a nature than my daughters who had been given very little.

I say we had to 'punish' the girl because—as I realised only in retrospect—there was an invisible point at which she had crossed the line separating a guest of the family from a child who was treated on the same terms as my own daughters. That is to say, my wife and I reprimanded her for exactly the same misdemeanours as the other two: lateness to the table, impertinence, getting up late, and so on. It became clear she was wholly unused to being treated as a normal child and subjected to steady and considered discipline of this kind. My wife and I were the more disappointed because the girl had seemed so much more mature than our second daughter. Now she was behaving as if she were much younger.

For my wife and myself, it was exactly like having a third child—and one who behaved worse than either of our real daughters had ever done. She lost her temper very quickly and answered us back, and when she was reprimanded, she stormed out of the room and then sulked for long periods. Yet at the same time she could be very sweet and affectionate, and not simply in order to gain what she wanted—though she was adept at using charm to that end.

When I say she was not used to being properly disciplined I do not mean she had not been disciplined at all. She was familiar with punishment, certainly, but punishment that was given more arbitrarily and perhaps more angrily than was the practice of my wife and myself.

She had told us at the beginning how badly the servant at her house had been treating her. My wife and I now began to wonder if there had not been more to say on the other side. We were starting to find out she was spiteful and demanding and devious beneath the surface charm.

* * *

Not having had an answer to my letter to her parents after two weeks, I decided it had not reached them and I should take another way to make contact. I would try to find someone at the store who could put me in touch with the father.

* * *

There was something that was worrying me. I had begun to notice that certain colleagues in the city's administration who belonged to the same minority as the girl, had ceased to appear at work. At first I assumed they had been reassigned to other departments. Nobody ever mentioned them or asked where they had gone. It was as if to raise those questions would have been in bad taste. Then gradually it became known by some mysterious process of osmosis that they had not been redeployed but dismissed.

* * *

The next Monday I went to the store after work and asked to speak to the manager. After dealing with some insolent subordinates who asked to know my business with him and then being kept waiting for twenty minutes, I was eventually led into the presence of someone I was told was a deputy-manager.

He was an oily little man with a ready but meaningless smile. I told him I had a personal message for the owner of the store. He looked surprised and when I uttered the name of the girl's father, he smiled and said: *I understand you now. That individual has had an interest in this company in the past.*

I asked him if that meant he was no longer the owner or part-owner, but he smiled affably and avoided answering my question.

I explained my attempts to contact him in the former capital, and he said nothing but tried to find out why I wanted to communicate with him. We had reached a courteous but granite-like impasse: I would not tell him my reason and he would not indicate whether or not he knew how to reach the girl's father. I left. The interview had lasted barely five minutes.

This was the day I first noticed posters around the city with warning references to health and hygiene and cleanliness. I paid them no attention at the time.

* * *

The next day, when I made my regular visit to the girl's house, I attempted to engage the servant in conversation.

I said: *Your young mistress is not always easy to cope with.*

She raised her eyes to heaven and said: *You want to watch out for her most of all when she's being nice. Those people know how to be very charming when they want something from you. But that little miss is a spiteful baggage when she doesn't get what she wants.*

I saw much truth in that. But her words also confirmed what the girl had said about the woman's mean-spiritedness.

* * *

That Friday I had an illustration of what the servant had warned me about.

I was in my study when the girl tapped at the door and came in. She shut it behind her and smiled at me. She had made herself up—as she often did in the evening despite my wife's disapproval—but this time she was wearing a frock I had never seen her in before. It was cut quite low and was very short and seemed to me positively indecent on a child of that age. She was either too old for it if it was a little girl's dress or she was too young if it was that of a grown woman.

She leant back against the door and said: *Do you like it? This is the frock Daddy likes to see me in most of all.*

I said it was very nice and resolved to speak to my wife about it.

She had come for her pocket-money. I gave her the usual sum—the same amount I gave to my younger girl—but she began to try to wheedle out of me more than I had agreed to give her. When she realised she was not going to get it, she lost her temper and went out slamming the door behind her.

* * *

My elder daughter's temper was not improved by hearing some bad news during the course of the following week. The city's College of Art and Design was not going to re-open this year because so many of its staff and students were still in prisoner-of-war camps or stranded in the Western Zone. That meant she would have to lower her sights and look for an apprenticeship in a dress-making establishment, though even that would not be easy to find now that prices were rising and cash was so short and luxuries were being dispensed with. I was a little worried by the reflection that the only people still buying tailored dresses were those who were benefitting from the Occupation: the toadying politicians and bureaucrats who were collaborating with the Enemy and the business-people who were profiting from the situation.

When I asked her if there was no other career she wished to pursue, she became upset and said: *You never respected my interest in couture. You never wanted me to do something so unacademic. You always wanted me to get better marks and you wouldn't accept that school-work bored me to death. Do you think I'm suddenly going to start studying again now?*

I had long ago resigned myself to the fact that she was not destined for a professional career. So I just said I wanted her to be happy and thought she should keep an open mind about other possibilities. I ended: *I think you should talk to your mother about it.*

She snapped: *Oh I know what she'll say. She'll say I didn't study hard enough for my school certificates. But whose fault is that?*

Her mother's second bout of ill-health had begun about a year after the birth of my younger daughter, when she was between two and three years old, and she had suffered badly from my wife's absence. But the more recent period of difficulty had occurred when she was fourteen and studying for important exams. She had seen her mother's slide into depression with obvious dismay. My wife had alternated between long periods of unresponsive silence and outbreaks of hysteria. So the girls had witnessed her bursting into tears for no apparent reason, losing her temper, and staying in her room all day. The elder child had had to take responsibility for her younger sister and, given her lack of academic ability, it was not surprising she had failed her exams so badly. My wife's illness had also had consequences for my own career.

My daughter seemed to believe her mother hated her and had deliberately tried to harm her prospects not only by disrupting her crucial exams but by denigrating her and lowering her expectations. They quarrelled frequently and bitterly and often for no good reason.

Seeing how the War and Occupation were reducing the opportunities for young people, I urged my daughter to consider other trades or crafts than couture. However, she ignored my advice and started looking for work as a trainee dress-maker. She quickly discovered how unlikely she was to find what she wanted in that uncertain economic climate.

* * *

It was now that I remembered my idea that the girl should give my elder daughter a gift. It would appeal to her love of shopping and the generosity that made giving presents enjoyable to her. So I began to conspire with her about the scheme, finding moments to raise it when my wife (who had disapproved of the idea) and the other girls were not around. We had several discussions about it in my study which I thought we had kept from them. That Saturday afternoon we went out together on some pretext and after a long and—to me—tedious process of evaluation and comparison, bought a beautiful scarf which I of course paid for.

The girl wrapped it very adroitly in some elegant paper we had purchased and that evening before supper she ceremoniously pre-sented it to my daughter. She said, as she and I had rehearsed, that it was something she had bought from the money saved up from the pocket-money I had given her.

I could see immediately that my daughter was displeased. She opened it and thanked the girl coldly. She said: *How intriguing. It's not at all my usual style.* The girl was crestfallen, and I think she realised that despite her outwardly courteous words, my daughter meant it was too old-fashioned and lacking in sophistication for her taste. And it emerged that, far from being grateful, she was resentful. She felt she was being patronised—that her irritation had been noticed and discussed and that this was a ploy to buy her goodwill. Later when she and I were alone she accused me of ar-ranging the whole thing in order to make her look petty-minded. And that night my wife reproved me for thinking that the taste of a girl of thirteen could be acceptable to our elder daughter. The scarf, she said, would have looked fine on either of the younger girls but is wholly inappropriate for a young woman of seventeen.

* * *

The girl had now been with us for nearly six weeks. During this time we had introduced her to visitors as a schoolfriend of our daughter and had not mentioned that she was living with us. Once or twice, however, friends visiting in the evening had realised she was a house-guest and to them we had just explained that she was staying with us overnight because her parents were away.

Because of the pressures of work and family, my wife and I did not have a very active social life. Occasionally we had friends round for little suppers. There was a man I had known from my time at the accountancy institute who came with his wife once or twice a year. And we dined now and then with my brother-in-law and his wife who lived in the city—though at some distance from our district.

One thing at least was in our favour, although we did not think of it as being of any importance at the time: it happened that the girl's given name was not one that would attract notice. Her surname, of course, was an entirely different matter since it not only pointed to her membership of the community but was an unusual one and therefore indicated a relationship with one of the city's most prominent businessmen.

The next Monday as I was coming down the stairs I met the joiner's wife who lived in one of the apartments on the floor below ours with her husband and their two small children. (Unfortunately the father of one of the couple—we never found out which—lived with them, and he was not a pleasant old man. My daughters had adopted a kitten about two years earlier which they allowed to play on the stairs and the old man had objected—wholly unreasonably—that it was noisy and dirty. One day it had simply disappeared, and we were all sure he was responsible.) We were on perfectly good terms with the young couple but the difference in age and status meant we had never progressed far beyond nods and greetings and occasional brief conversations.

On this occasion the wife smiled and asked me who 'the new little girl' was whom she saw so often coming and going. Without thinking, I said she was my wife's niece.

Why had I not just said that she was a schoolfriend of my younger daughter? I suppose I felt that the neighbours would see her more often than occasional visitors would, and they would realise she was living with us. To say that she was a young relative raised fewer questions and seemed less in need of elaboration than if I had continued to call her a friend of my daughter.

I mentioned to my wife what had happened, and she laughed and said she had told the tailor's wife that the girl was *my* niece. We thought it was amusing but we agreed we should say the same thing if anyone asked.

So that evening over supper I asked the others what each of them had been saying about the girl's connection with us. They had all referred to her as a friend of the younger child. In that case, I pointed out, we had probably aroused curiosity on the part of our neighbours by telling different stories. We would have to say she was a relative and was also at the same school as our daughter.

My elder daughter said: *Does it matter? She's not going to be here much longer. Who cares whether she's a friend or a relative?*

I'm sure we were all wondering how much longer she would be with us.

I said: *You're right and it probably doesn't matter. But we don't want our neighbours to gossip about us. The way things are going, nobody knows what's likely to happen.*

I didn't want to alarm them by saying any more, but I was afraid that under the Occupation, the authorities were likely to become more and more intrusive. We were already on thin ice by failing to inform the school of the girl's new address.

It was clear we could not go back on the account we had given the neighbours without making them suspicious. At that juncture my clever younger daughter pointed out that one of my cousins had a daughter who had the same given name as the girl. In that case since 'cousin' and 'niece' were fairly close in meaning, could we not say she was that girl? I said nothing to the others but reflected it had the advantage that if anyone should ever check my story, it would be found that I did indeed have a cousin of that name. (The fact was that my cousin was then a little over thirty, but that might not matter if she were not too closely investigated.) The younger girls thought it was hilarious and treated it as a game.

My elder daughter looked annoyed and said: *Nobody will believe we're related to her.*

The younger asked indignantly: *Whyever not?*

Her sister just said: *It's obvious.*

To cover an awkward moment I said: *That's decided then. We'll say to people in the building that she is not the niece of either of us but the daughter of a cousin of mine and that your mother and I call her our niece for the sake of simplicity.*

I was the more concerned to get our story right because something was making me uneasy at this stage. The wireless had picked up the theme of the posters and was emphasising the issue of health and the need for what it called the 'decontamination' of the nation's source of infection. I had a feeling that I knew what that was about.

* * *

About now it became clear that the two younger girls were not getting on at all. At the week-ends tensions rose because we were all at home, and I realised my wife was not able to ensure harmony between the two children—and I suppose that was because of her emotional involvement. She often bent over backwards not to favour her own child and her indulgence towards the girl occasionally annoyed our younger daughter. I was slow to realise how much it also irritated our elder child.

The problem of keeping the girl entertained became more and more acute. She was clearly too young for my elder daughter to take under her wing, and as for my younger girl, the difficulty was that she had quite different interests. She loved to read, to play the piano, and to listen to concerts on the wireless, and none of those pastimes held any appeal for the girl. (Although her technical proficiency on the piano was high, she derived no pleasure from music and after the first few weeks rarely played unless my wife or I urged her to. And she knew only the most sugary and superficial waltzes.) Since the two younger girls had such different personalities and interests, my daughter's friends and the girl had nothing in common either. So when my daughter visited them at their houses or had them round to our apartment, she did not want the girl to join them. She insisted the girl was a bore and a drag on their enjoyment because she prattled nonstop about her exciting life with her own friends, which irritated the others.

My daughter's friends were much sharper and more inquisitive about the world than the girl and although they were fascinated by makeup and fashion and Hollywood actresses, they had numerous other interests. Moreover, they had a sense of humour while the girl appeared to have none.

* * *

It was on the Thursday of that week while we were having supper that something happened which made relations between the younger children deteriorate more rapidly. The girl was, as she so often did, boasting about her family's country-house and the lavish picnics her mother organised there in the summer.

My younger daughter said: *Perhaps we'll all be there with you next summer.*

Oh no, the girl said. *Mummy only invites friends and people who work with Daddy.*

But my father might be working with yours by then, she persevered. The girl's mouth fell open.

I said quickly: *It's just a possibility. I work in accountancy and your father might offer me employment.*

The girl looked shocked and said: *But even if that happened, we never entertain Daddy's employees.* (She spoke the word with evident distaste.) *Only his business associates.*

I didn't mind her being so dismissive towards me, but my younger daughter reacted as if she had been struck on the mouth.

She fell silent—always a bad sign with her—but I saw her watching the girl closely while she chattered on.

After a while my daughter interrupted her and said: *I hate swimming in lakes. They're so cold. When we go to the capital every autumn we swim in a lovely warm pool.*

The girl stared at her in contempt: *A swimming pool? Public swimming baths? I've never been to one of those and I know I should hate it.*

My younger daughter snapped: *Well, you won't be there anyway. We won't want you there any more than we want you here now.*

That sort of remark was very untypical of her. The girl flushed and lowered her head.

I said: *That was a very unkind thing to say. And quite untrue.* I hesitated but felt I had to go further. I said to the girl: *We like having you here. Of course we do.*

The words sounded hollow even to me. Nobody said anything. The girl kept her head down. When I could see her face again, her eyes were brimming with tears.

Something changed after that incident. From that moment on, my younger daughter never listened to the girl's boasts with the same rapt expression.

* * *

All this time the girl had not encountered our domestic again (having met her at dinner on her first visit) since she was out at the times when the woman was working at the apartment. Every weekday the two children and I set off after breakfast to catch the 8.04 tram (in their case) and the 8.08 one (in mine) from the tram-stop around the corner. That meant they left before the domestic arrived and she had always gone when they got back. But, of course, she could see from the things in the girls' bedroom that there was a second child lodging with us. We had no reason to hide it from her, though I suggested to my wife that she just say 'a schoolfriend' had moved in for a while and not mention that it was the girl whom she had already encountered on the occasion when she had stayed late to serve dinner. My wife agreed.

Then the day after the quarrel about the swimming-pool, I arrived home earlier than usual because I had a headache, to find my wife and the domestic in the kitchen arguing about the money the woman had spent buying our groceries. She had worked for us for two years and although she was industrious and cheerful, we were increasingly unhappy with her because my wife suspected her of stealing food and even cheating her on the occasions when she did the shopping. We would have got rid of her except that our younger daughter was fond of her and she was a very good cook. Now my wife was insisting she could not have spent so much and she was demanding more change. When I arrived, they explained to me that they had been checking the cost of the groceries and did not agree on the calculation of the bill.

The domestic greeted me with the words: *Will you do the adding up, sir? After all, you're an accountant.*

I did as I was asked and found my wife was in the wrong. The domestic had spent precisely the amount she claimed. My wife was furious with me and charged out of the room. I chatted to the woman in order to make up for my wife's failure to apologise for the unfair accusation she had made. That meant the domestic stayed later than usual and was only preparing to leave as the girl got back from school. She was alone because my younger daughter had her ballet class on Fridays.

Now that the girl and the domestic had encountered each other at last, the woman reacted as if the matter were of no significance and just smiled and said: *I thought it was probably you, dear.*

I left them chatting in the hall and went to our bedroom to see how my wife was. As I entered, she turned from the dressing-table where she was sitting and said sarcastically: *After all, you're an accountant, sir.*

I said softly: *I'm all but a fully certified accountant.*

She said: *But you're not because you never passed the exams and if you had, how much better off we'd be.*

She spoke loudly and I shushed her with my finger and opened the door to look into the hall. It was empty but I heard voices from the kitchen and quietly approached the door and looked round it. The girl and the domestic were sitting at the table talking animatedly. I had never seen the girl looking so relaxed and happy.

I went back to the bedroom and closed the door. My wife was still angry. She said: *You condemned us to live like this because you failed your exams.*

I said: *And whose fault is that?*

I shouldn't have said that. She gasped and turned away, her hand across her mouth.

The fact that she had become unwell after the birth of our first child meant I had been preoccupied with looking after both of them and as a result, I had failed my professional exams. It had not happened because of any choice of hers, and I had never felt resentment towards her for harming my career like that—though it was sometimes hard to take her complaints that I earned so little when her own weakness had been the cause.

I tried to withdraw my unfortunate remark, but it was too late. She said: *You throw that in my face as if I wanted to be ill just to spite you.*

Now I was angry that she had rebuffed my attempt to apologise. I said: *Of course you didn't choose to become ill but you did get ill and everything followed from that, and all I'm saying is that means you don't have the right to accuse me of failing. Nobody could have coped better than I did under those circumstances.*

Those circumstances! she repeated. *The circumstances were as good as they could be. My father had given you this apartment. We weren't paying any rent. We could have afforded proper help with the baby if you hadn't made such a mess of our finances.*

I tried to keep my voice down, but my wife was shouting by now.

I heard the front-door shut behind the domestic, so at least she wouldn't hear, but it worried me that the girl might be able to catch some of what my wife was saying.

* * *

What my wife was so upset about was something that made our situation much less advantageous than it should have been. If I had been fully qualified, things would not have been as bad at work as they were because I would have secured a higher position in the Department of Finance and therefore would have been less vulnerable. Even before the Occupation, my circumstances were unenviable. Now everything became worse because of a sudden new development at work. And I dared not share my fears with my wife since signs that she was not entirely herself had emerged during that quarrel which ominously reminded me of the onset of her previous periods of ill health.

It is true that my employment in the department was in name as a mere book-keeper—a post far below what my qualifications entitled me to since I was all but fully certified as an accountant. What my wife failed to realise was that I was doing the work of a fully qualified accountant even though I was not receiving the appropriate salary. My relations with the people I worked with had never been good. The head of my section was a bully and a boor, and his deputy was the same but in a much more devious way. They were both less qualified and less educated than I, and they recognised and resented that.

Now that the Enemy had installed a brutal puppet dictatorship to rule our country, advancement was not by merit but by obedience and flattery so the foulest scum bubbled to the surface, and my two superiors were among the worst: nasty, spiteful, bullying, and exploitative. They had already inflicted a series of petty humiliations on me whenever they had the chance. I believed they disliked me because I refused to tell smutty jokes and was an excellent time-keeper. All of that made me, in their eyes, a self-righteous prig. I had worked there for five years, and although my record was impeccable, I was under constant threat of dismissal. The fear that the head and his deputy inspired in their subordinates meant that few of us trusted each other. There was nobody there I liked with the single exception of the man who shared my office and whom I thought of as a friend.

The fact I was disliked upset me a great deal. I used to try to persuade myself that I was just unlucky to have such unpleasant superiors and colleagues. But I could not avoid asking myself if the problem arose with me. Was it something in my personality that was the reason why I was not on good terms with them? Would another person employed in my place have got on better? I believed that was quite likely. I knew why I was considered self-righteous by my colleagues—and especially by the head and his deputy. Part of the problem was that I just could not engage in the back-slapping and dirty jokes that all the other men went in for. Above all, I did not take part in the 'teasing' of the female secretaries and could not conceal my disapproval of that practice. Some of the banter and the practical jokes were cruel, and more than once I saw a young woman run out of the room in tears while the men roared with laughter. So I knew it was in part my own fastidiousness and refusal to countenance such behaviour that made me unpopular. I consoled myself with that reflection and with the fact that my colleagues— both my superiors and my equals—nearly all disliked each other. There were a few friendships amongst them, but they were more like alliances based on common interests than true friendships, and they tended to be temporary.

There was a big noisy bar near the office, and most of the people in my department went there after work. I patronised it just occasionally and only if my friendly colleague was going. I talked mostly to him, and I was always the first to set off for home. He and I had one of those work friendships which are not tested outside that context and which, if they are, often reveal themselves to be too shallow to survive.

About now I stopped going to the bar altogether for several reasons, all of which were the result of the Occupation: the price of the drinks had risen; the deterioration in public transport meant it took longer to get home; and because we had an increasing work-load, we were getting out of the office later and later.

* * *

During the course of that week there was a sudden new development at work. The change in our nation's circumstances had both
altered and hugely increased our responsibilities. Until the invasion,
the Department of Finance did what every such unit in a city administration does: in the simplest terms, we supervised the raising
of the local taxes that had been decreed by the elected councillors
and then allocated expenditure to the different departments in ac-
cordance with the policy formulated by the councillors. Those men
had very swiftly been replaced by officials chosen by the occupation
authority, and for a while nothing much had changed. Now, however, we were being asked to perform a wide range of new functions
in order to raise money for the occupying power's war effort. New
taxes were introduced and that created a huge amount of work, and
yet we were not allowed to take on more staff.

Although virtually none of us was happy to be helping the
Enemy, we accepted that was part of the new order of things. As I
have said, however, a new issue had begun to present itself that was
making me very uneasy.

That Wednesday I and all my colleagues on my level were summoned to the office of my head of section, and we found him there
with his deputy. He told us an announcement was about to be made
that all members of the community to which the girl belonged who
were living in the city and appeared to possess wealth over a certain
figure were being put on a 'list'. They would have to come forward
to declare themselves and make a return of their assets by a certain
date which was three months away. Anyone who failed to do so by
that time would be punished. Our task would be to work on those
returns to compile a set of accounts for each individual. We asked
no questions because we knew we would receive no answers, and
in that climate, even to put a question was to place one's loyalty in
doubt.

I was now very worried. The girl's father was surely one of the
wealthiest men in the community and so should be on the list.

Given that he was absent and out of contact, he would not be able to put himself on it, but someone else surely would do so, and that would lead to enquiries about his and his family's whereabouts.

* * *

When I got home the last thing I wanted was to have to hear about an unpleasant incident, but I found my wife very upset and had to listen to the whole story. She explained that the girl had gone to the dentist that afternoon and instead of going back to school, which she would have reached as it was ending, she had come home. She had therefore encountered our domestic. All three had been talking amicably enough in the kitchen when the woman had made a very mild remark to the girl: *You've noticed we're making a special dish for you because you won't eat what everyone else is having this evening? Do you think it's kind of you to put the mistress to so much trouble just because you won't eat certain things?*

The girl had reacted with instant anger and said: *Oh, you've got the interests of this family at heart. I know that very well.*

She appeared to be speaking with some sarcastic veiled meaning, but the domestic had not risen to the bait and had merely smiled and said: *You're quite right, dear. I do.*

As if goaded by the domestic's unruffled response, the girl had then said: *You can't pull the wool over my eyes. I'm not as stupid as you think.*

My wife had no idea what she meant and the domestic appeared equally puzzled but wholly unconcerned. It was time for her to go and so the subject was dropped.

When they were alone, my wife had asked the girl what she had meant. She had said: *I know exactly what those people are like. I've had experience of them.*

This left my wife none the wiser, but the girl would say no more.

Talking it over, my wife and I decided the most likely explanation was that the girl was accusing the domestic of cheating us or stealing. She was already under suspicion.

* * *

Later that evening I learned something that placed the day's events at the office in a larger context. When the others had gone to bed, I tuned the wireless to the station broadcasting from our former capital in the Western Zone. I sometimes did that in order to learn the fate of that part of our poor conquered nation.

It was announced that overnight the whole apparatus of laws on what was called 'ethnic hygiene' had been introduced in the Western Zone. I knew more about that than most of my compatriots. Before the War our rulers had tried to stay on friendly terms with the Enemy. Our government's complete control of the press and wireless ensured that our citizens had been told nothing of the crimes that were being carried out in the Enemy's country. However, I understood their language fairly well and occasionally listened to their broadcasts and therefore knew of the regime's deep hostility towards the girl's community. For several years it had been enacting legislation that required people to prove they did not belong to it and if they failed, isolated them from the rest of the nation. If those laws were now being applied in the Western Zone, I was sure it would only be a short time before they were introduced into our Eastern Zone.

* * *

I lay awake late that night thinking about the situation. I was concerned about the fact my younger daughter was being seen to arrive with the girl every morning at school—though they then parted to attend different classes—and to meet her at the end of the day and walk to the tram-stop together. If anyone took an interest in the girl, that link would quickly become apparent. In the morning I told my wife what I had decided. Because of my worries about her health, I didn't tell her what my real fears were but gave her the justification I had prepared for the children.

At breakfast I announced I had decided that my daughter should take an earlier tram to school than the usual one which the girl would continue to take. And at the end of the day, that would be repeated: the girl should wait for a later one to bring her home.

Of course, my daughter was horrified at the idea of having to leave the house ten minutes earlier and the girl was not very happy at having to hang around for ten minutes longer after lessons.

They demanded to know why I was imposing this regime. I said to the girl: *It's simply that we don't want the school to realise that you are not living with your parents. If you arrive and leave every day with the same fellow-pupil instead of your family's servant, someone will become curious.*

They accepted that and agreed to the new timetable. My daughter hurried out of the house to catch the earlier tram.

* * *

The next day the requirement was broadcast on the nine o'clock news that wealthy members of the girl's community must come forward and detail their assets. It was also announced that after the deadline had passed, a reward would be given to anyone suggesting the name of an individual who had improperly failed to declare himself.

That made it pretty well certain that if the girl's father somehow avoided being on the list, someone would denounce him.

* * *

The following Monday afternoon I was buying some cigars in a shop near my office when I ran into a former colleague and we chatted for a while. He had worked in my section but, being ambitious and, I have to say, just a shade devious, he had managed to secure a higher post in another part of the Department of Finance about a year earlier. He now told me he had succeeded in gaining a transfer to something called the Department of Protection because of the fine opportunities for career advancement offered by 'the new situation'.

I told him I had not heard of it, and he explained that its creation had not yet been announced. A new 'Ministry of Protection' was to be created nationally with a corresponding 'Department of Protection' in each city. The function of these new institutions was the safeguarding of the minority community and their assets.

I didn't pay it a great deal of attention because there had already been a stream of such orders dealing with various groups: Catholics, Protestants, Romanies, Communist party-members, ex-servicemen, prisoners-of-war, and so on. It seemed just another tiresome piece of bureaucracy.

* * *

I hardly had time to think about that, when I found I had to deal with a crisis at home. As soon as I walked into the apartment, my wife told me what had happened about an hour earlier.

My younger daughter arrived on the earlier tram and the girl got back ten minutes later. My daughter was with her mother in the kitchen, and they heard her going into the bedroom. Then the girl uttered a terrible scream. When my wife and daughter rushed to find out what was the matter, they discovered her staring at her oriental doll. It was lying on the floor with its beautiful china face smashed and the clothes covered in paint of various colours. The girl was almost hysterical. She said she had entered the room and found it like that with a pillow on top of it. By the time I arrived, the apartment was in uproar. The two girls were screaming at each other, both in tears. The girl shouted at my daughter that she had done it. She angrily denied the charge and said she had not even been into the room since she got back. It escalated from there and my daughter cried: *Why don't you just go away? Nobody wants you here.*

The girl's chin was wobbling as she said: *Your parents have been kind to me. They like having me here even if you don't.*

My daughter replied: *No, they don't. They hate you like we all do. We've only been nice to you because your daddy's rich and might give mine a better job.*

That provoked such a screwed up, intense, angry look on the girl's face that I felt the first feelings of alarm. She said: *No he won't. He'll be so angry at the way you've treated me, he'll get his revenge on all of you.* She ran out of the room.

My wife suggested that the destruction of the doll had happened by accident. That was just remotely possible since the thing was sometimes left on the shelf above where the girl said she had found it. However, it seemed unlikely that a fall from that height—even onto the bare boards near the wall—would have broken its face into so many fragments. And the presence of the paint was hard to explain as an accident. The girls had been using watercolours the previous day and had mixed some in little pots. But they had not been left on the floor where the doll had apparently fallen onto them, and even if that had occurred, it was difficult to see how the paint had so thoroughly smeared the doll's garments. Above all, even assuming the doll had been left on the shelf and the paints somehow positioned below it, why had the doll fallen? Even slamming the door of the room should not have dislodged it, and nobody had had any reason to open or close the door during the day. And if it had been covered by a pillow, how had that got there?

My wife told me she was convinced the girl had done it herself to cause trouble. She insisted that there had been a delay of at least a minute between her going into the bedroom and the scream. Why had she taken so long to notice something that was so obvious?

I was sceptical she could have done it in so short a time.

In that case, my wife argued, she did it this morning after our daughter had left for the tram. She had a good ten minutes.

If that were true, the doll had been lying there undiscovered all day. My wife could not recall if she had happened to look into the room. It was not the day on which the domestic cleaned it, and so she would have had no reason to go in while she was working at the apartment earlier that day.

The girl insisted our daughter had done it immediately after getting home, but my wife was certain that, as she herself said, she had not even gone into the bedroom but had come straight to the kitchen.

My elder daughter returned just in time for supper. She could throw no light on the matter since she had left the house shortly after the girls and had been out all day looking for work and meeting friends.

It occurred to me that another possibility was that the domestic had done it, but I could not imagine what motive she might have had. I decided not to voice my suspicion to my wife.

The value of the doll had been utterly destroyed. What was surprising was that the girl seemed to become fonder of it than before. I had expected her to have thrown it away since she was far too old to play with such toys. On the contrary, she now became inseparable from it. She removed the few fragments of the face that remained and took off the spoiled clothes and threw them away. The doll was now a faceless stuffed figure in brown fabric and yet she treasured it and kept it with her much of the time, as if afraid someone would steal it from her even though it was now worthless.

* * *

The regime of staggered arrivals and departures for the two girls was only in force for a short time and that was because just two days after the incident with the doll, the authorities revealed their plans for our Eastern Zone. As my former colleague had told me, a new entity called the 'Ministry of Protection' was created to look after the interests of people like the girl, and a representative of it was being formed within our city administration.

The following evening it was announced on the nine o'clock news that the new 'Department of Protection' had been set up, and its first directive was that all schools were required to look at the identity-card of every child and report to the department any whose names or addresses indicated that they were members of the 'protected community'. Children in that category would be given the chance to attend a school at which they could study their own culture, and plans were in hand to set up a network of such institutions. Until then they would not be required to attend existing places of learning and that 'guidance'—as it was called—was to take immediate effect.

* * *

On Monday, therefore, our younger daughter went to school alone while the girl stayed at home all day.

When I got back that evening my wife told me what had happened when the domestic arrived for work and saw the girl. When she heard why she was not at school, she said: *Do you want to put on a spare pinny and help me do the living-room?*

And to my wife's surprise, the girl had taken the pinafore from her and tied it on. That spoiled lazy creature who could not be induced to keep her own part of the bedroom tidy! My wife had told her to take it off and explained to the domestic that she was a guest and could not be expected to do housework.

My wife said to me later that at least it would have kept her busy since she had just sat around the whole day doing her nails, tinkling on the piano, and browsing through our elder daughter's fashion magazines.

At first the girl was delighted not to have to go to lessons. And she talked—tactlessly, I thought—of how excited she was at the prospect of going to a school where she would meet her friends again. (I suppose she was assuming that the children of wealthy members of her community would choose to leave their schools in the former capital and return here to attend one of the new schools since they could live at home. But I knew that if they had been in the capital when the invasion occurred, they would not have been able to get back.)

I felt responsible for the girl, and so I told my younger daughter that until she started at her new school, she should teach her in the

evening the things she had learned that day and do her homework
with her. Both girls were dismayed by the idea, but my daughter
made a good attempt. It didn't work, and they merely bickered and
squabbled at the dining-table after supper for a couple of hours. My
daughter complained to me that the girl was too stupid to understand anything. After a week I took over and tried to do it myself,
and I had as little success as my daughter. It wasn't that the girl was
stupid exactly—in some respects she was quite clever, or perhaps I
should say cunning because it was always when her own interests
were involved that she was most acute. But she had no desire to
learn anything whose usefulness to her she could not immediately
see. However, I persevered with her studies.

Since it was embarrassing for both of us to have the others
listening as we sat at the table—especially my younger daughter
whose mocking, mischievous face I often caught looking in our
direction when the girl was being particularly slow-witted—after a
few days I took her into my study for her lessons so that we would
not be overheard.

* * *

By now the lists of wealthy members of the girl's community had
begun to be distributed. Each list had between five and ten names
and was numbered and then given to one of us. I received mine
now and it was number '3'. We had to produce a complete set of accounts for each of the individuals named. We were ordered to keep
the list and the corresponding accounts carefully locked up since
they were highly confidential.

By this time my wife had begun to find the girl's presence in
the house all day a serious nuisance. She complained that when she
had gone shopping, the girl had insisted on trailing along with her.
And that had been tiresome when she had met her friends in a café
for a gossip of the kind that would be inhibited by the presence of
a thirteen-year-old.

Our elder daughter took no responsibility for the girl. She was mostly either in her room playing records or out visiting girl-friends or roaming around the city asking for work at dress-shops and occasionally being given a day or two of cutting and sewing.

The lessons I was giving the girl weren't going well. By that time of the evening I was tired, but the girl had been cooped up all day and was bored and restless. Although she disliked learning, the hour she spent with me was a kind of high point of her day, and she dressed specially for it in the frock she said her father liked. She would sit very close to me, and I could smell the expensive perfume she had brought from home.

Things weren't helped by the fact that my wife kept bursting into the room. It became intolerable. She was doing it three or four times in the course of the hour and with the flimsiest pretexts: *Did we want something to drink? Were we too cold?*

The girl would say something like: *Thank you, but we're fine as we are.* And my wife would take that badly and flounce out.

* * *

When I came home on Friday evening I found that all was not well. The girl was sulking in her room and my wife was fuming in the living-room. I soon heard the story. They had gone into the centre to shop, and the girl had got on her nerves with her constant demands for attention or money to buy trinkets and with her unwillingness to walk more than a few yards without pestering her to take a taxi or at least a tram.

That night when we were going to bed my wife told me she wanted to send the girl back to her own house where she would be perfectly comfortable being looked after by the servant. I pointed out that she got on with the woman extremely badly. My wife remained unconvinced, and I told her that in my weekly meetings with the woman during the last few weeks I had become convinced she was an extremely unpleasant person and not someone to whose care a child should be entrusted. My wife responded that was unfortunate but it was no concern of ours. The girl's parents had chosen to leave the servant in charge of her, and we were not justified in questioning their decision.

I said that sending her back now would undo all the good we had done by looking after her. When her parents returned she would not tell them how well we had treated her. Instead, she would complain about us—if she even mentioned us at all—and describe how we had driven her away for no good reason. My wife was obdurate and insisted that our paramount obligation was to our own children, whose peace of mind was now being threatened by the girl's presence.

I said that although we had not taken her in simply because we hoped to gain some favour from her father, at the same time we should not lightly throw away that possibility. Times were uncertain and given that my job was poorly paid and my hold on it insecure, it would be rash to abandon what might be a chance of being offered a better position. We had already expended a not inconsiderable sum on her food and other expenses and if we abandoned her, her father would be unlikely to refund me for my expenses on his daughter's behalf.

Then my wife brought up the fact that I was now teaching the girl. I thought at first that she was thinking merely of my interests, and I admitted I was always tired in the evenings and wanted simply to relax with the newspaper in front of the wireless. But it turned out that wasn't my wife's main concern. Part of it was that she felt I was neglecting my own children and in danger of arousing their jealousy by devoting so much time and attention to the girl. Especially, she said, when I was shut up in a room with her away from the rest of the family. I agreed to discontinue the lessons. Having won this point, my wife relented and consented to let the girl stay. She said that our domestic had got on well with her and the solution might be, after all, to consign the girl to her custody during the hours she was working in the apartment.

* * *

When I told the girl the next morning that there would be no more lessons, she was surprisingly disappointed given how uninterested in learning she had always been.

The week-end passed with less friction than usual and on Monday, when the domestic arrived, the girl put on a pinafore and followed the woman around the apartment helping with the house-work—or at least believing she was being useful—and chattering nineteen to the dozen. When my younger daughter got back from school, she joined the two of them in preparing the evening meal or baking cakes. The only time when the two younger girls were not quarrelling during this period was when they were working to-gether under the supervision of the domestic.

* * *

Then a week or so later another means of occupying the girl and keeping her out of my wife's hair appeared. On Tuesday evening when I got home, my wife told me that as she and the girl were setting off for the shops that morning, they had met the joiner's wife on the landing below with her two small children. The girl had made a great fuss of them, and the good-natured young woman had invited her to come in tomorrow evening and help her bath them and put them to bed. She had responded with great enthusiasm: *I'd love to.*

My wife thought it was an excellent idea. It would get the girl out of the apartment for a couple of hours and give us all a much-needed break at a time when we four family members were all together. I agreed, but after dinner I took the girl into my study and made her sit down. I issued a solemn warning that she must re-veal absolutely nothing about herself to anyone in that family. They knew her first name and her age and beyond that they must know nothing at all: her family's name, the part of town where she lived, or the nature of her father's work. She looked puzzled and I explained that her father's surname was unusual and if her relationship to him became known, since he was a very prominent businessman in the city, it might create awkwardness. The joiner and his wife were very poor while her family was very rich. It was better not to let them know how great the disparity in their circumstances was.

All of that was true, but I was also worried that her surname would betray her membership of the community. I knew that the old man, who was the father of either the joiner or his wife, had nasty views about politics, and I didn't want to give him anything to get his teeth into. I had heard him once or twice, as I passed his landing, holding forth about foreigners coming into our country and buying up our houses and businesses, and I was pretty sure he would have a particularly strong prejudice against the 'protected community'.

The next evening the girl made her first visit to the joiner's apartment and a couple of hours later came back in a more cheerful mood than I had seen for weeks. We asked her how she had got on and she said: *The little girl is adorable. And the boy is about the same age as my brother and reminds me of him so much.*

I thought for a moment she had gone mad because I was thinking of her brother who was believed to be in a prisoner-of-war camp and had forgotten that she had another one who was much younger than her.

It was clear that she and the joiner's wife had become friends, and it seemed strange that a girl who was so self-obsessed and loved to be the centre of attention should be so fond of small children who are demanding in just the same way.

From now on the girl went down to the other apartment every evening and was often late to the dinner-table. None of us minded and it felt very good to be alone as a family once again.

For one thing, we were able to release our pent-up irritation at the girl's boastfulness or laugh at her misunderstandings. One evening about two weeks after she had started visiting the apartment below and while she was still there, my younger daughter told us how she had asked her: *Don't your parents go out in the evenings? I've never seen them dress up and set off somewhere.* She had gone on to say that most evenings her mother and father put on evening-clothes and went out and she did not see them again that day. And it appeared that she saw very little of them at all because her father had usually left for work by the time she had breakfast and her mother never appeared before midday, by which time—at least on weekdays—the girl was at school.

I was so intrigued by this that when she joined us a little later, I asked her about it. She was only too happy to chatter about her parents' glamorous lives. It became apparent that she very rarely shared the evening meal with them in the way that we four always did. She and her younger brother ate much earlier and in a separate room—the nursery?—and it was a special treat for her to eat in the dining-room on the rare occasions when her parents were neither dining out nor entertaining guests at home. The only time she spent with her mother was in the early evening, when she would sometimes chat to her while she was getting dressed with the help of her maid.

And where do your parents go every evening? I asked. *Do they go out to dinner at friends' houses?*

Sometimes, she said. But most often they dined at restaurants or the Casino, which was in the city's grandest hotel, and then they usually went on to a night-club. Occasionally she was woken very late by the sound of their return.

I said nothing to her, of course, but as my wife and I agreed afterwards, it seemed a neglectful way to treat your children. I had thought her parents were people to look up to, but from what the girl was telling us, that was not the case at all.

* * *

One night a few days later, as we were getting ready for bed, my wife told me about an incident she had witnessed that afternoon. The girl had been 'helping' the domestic and had done something stupid and been reprimanded. Instantly she had flared up and said: *You have no right to speak to me like that. You're just a paid employee.*

What it illustrated was that she, who had mostly been left in the care of servants, had not been taught to accept from them the kind of authority that a parent had.

The domestic, my wife said, had taken this abuse very well and just smiled.

* * *

All this time I was in doubt whether my wife's suspicion that our domestic was cheating her was justified or was the consequence of her highly-strung state.

One evening at supper a day or two later, my elder daughter was talking about the people who worked at a place where she did occasional jobs. She told us about one of them being caught pilfering from the shop. To my surprise the girl started to boast with astonishing frankness of how she had learned how to detect dishonesty on the part of her parents' servants. I managed to get her alone afterwards and I said: *That was very interesting. Tell me, how would you behave once you had discovered that a servant was stealing?*

A look of feral cunning came over her face. She said: *Have you any particular reason for asking me that?*

Of course I had to say I hadn't. But the incident made me wonder if the girl had detected our domestic in such an act and had been using it to manipulate and blackmail her. That would explain why the woman had damaged the doll—it had been an act of revenge. If I was right, she hated the girl, although she concealed that hatred very effectively. In that case, her apparently good-natured response to the girl's nastiness, in the spat my wife had described, was because she dared not quarrel with her for fear that the girl would reveal her pilfering. And that hypothesis explained the remark the girl had made: *You can't pull the wool over my eyes.*

As a consequence of this incident, I became more sympathetic to my wife's suggestion that we should dismiss the domestic. We couldn't tolerate a situation in which our servant was in the power of the girl.

An even more pressing motive was that money was getting tighter. The steep rise in the price of basic commodities—bread, coal, transport—was aggravated by the fact that the girl was costing us a lot. There was her food and because of her faddishness—which we accommodated as far as we could afford to—her subsistence was a heavier charge than that of either of our daughters. We had to buy her new clothes because she refused to wear anything that had belonged to our younger daughter although they were the same size. I now told my wife that had to stop.

I had my schedule of how much extra she was costing us: so much for her food, for her pocket-money, her clothing, her tram-fares, and so on. I looked forward to presenting it to her father and receiving not only a refund but also an expression of his grati-tude when he saw how much I had spent on his daughter and how carefully my wife and I had looked after her. So up to a point, the higher the figure the happier I was, but I could not help worry-ing that there was no knowing how long it would be before I was reimbursed.

* * *

The following week on Wednesday evening we were listening to the nine o'clock news—the nine o'clock lies as I called it to my wife because it was nothing but propaganda on behalf of the occupying power—when we heard that the laws of ethnic hygiene which had already come into force in the Western Zone, were now being en-acted in our zone. (Since we now had no parliament or legitimate government, new legislation was simply announced by the collabo-rationist regime.) As was usual with such edicts, the laws came into force at midnight.

I watched the girl's face, and she showed no emotion at all. She obviously had no idea how much of a threat to her and her family this represented.

I realised I would have to find the time to do the paperwork that would protect me, since one of the effects was that everyone working for the state or municipality had to produce a certificate showing that both their parents and at least three of their grandparents had been baptised in a church belonging to one or other Christian denomination within a year of their birth. Anyone who could not do that was automatically dismissed. The deadline for the production of such a certificate was two months away, and so that very evening I had to start finding out where six of my forebears had been born and christened. Luckily I had most of the information I needed.

I finished my letters to the relevant parish-clerks after midnight—long after all the girls had gone to bed. Knowing that thousands of people would be making the same requests in the next few days, I went down to the street and put my letters into a post-box on the corner. When I got back my wife had retired to rest, but when I went into our room I found she was still awake. I told her I was afraid that the rule about baptismal records would be extended and that before long not just employees of the state but everybody would be required to show on their identity-card that they did not have even one non-Christian grandparent.

Since all the parish-clerks in the country had been deluged with enquiries, it was two weeks before I received a positive response from all of them, and then I had to send a money-order to pay for a copy of the relevant entry.

I had to take those documents to an office to have them registered. Each visit required several hours of waiting in a queue. That office then sent them back to each parish for verification, and when I had received word that my certificates had been authenticated, I had to take my identity-card back and have it stamped. In my case it was endorsed with the legend 'Four-quarters Christian'. I completed all of that only a few days before the deadline.

Within a few days of the announcement, several of my colleagues stopped coming to work, and I assumed they knew they would be unable to provide the documentation required. I hoped they had found other employment—though how long they would be able to work at all seemed problematical to me.

* * *

It was now—perhaps because she was missing them more and more—that the girl began to talk with greater frankness about her family. That Friday at supper she mentioned the frequent arguments between her father and her brother. Her brother was out most of the latter part of the day and often came in very late at night—if at all—and then blundered up the stairs and slammed his door. She hesitated and then said: *Once when he had drunk too much he came into my room.* She seemed to be going to say more but stopped. She wrinkled her nose. Then she went on: *Whenever he came in drunk, the next morning he would stay in bed until lunch-time.* With a prim moue of distaste she said, clearly quoting her father, *he drinks with the dog-catcher's mate.* He showed no interest in the business their father had built up *by the sweat of his brow and the calluses on his hands.* Instead he wanted to be a painter. And with a knowing look the girl commented: *The only people who make money from painting have a brush in one hand and a ladder in the other.*

When she spoke like that, I could almost hear her father's voice: boorish, foul-mouthed, angry.

It emerged from what she was saying that her brother and their father quarrelled fiercely and frequently about the boy's behaviour and about the meagreness of the allowance his father gave him, which did not allow him to keep up with the sons of his father's business associates in the city. And they argued about his father's refusal to let him go to art-school and to fund his education as a painter. When the government had issued its request for volunteers to join the reserves, the young man had announced he was going to join the army and his parents had been horrified. The girl said: *He only joined up in order to thumb his nose at our father.*

My wife and I agreed later that the girl's father sounded as if he might not be the kind of man who would be grateful to us for what we had done for his child.

* * *

All this time, I was trying to find out if the girl's father was on any of the lists of the wealthy. By now, due to the carelessness of my colleagues who left their work on their desk when they went out for lunch, I had managed to look at everything relating to lists Nos. 1 and 2. The name I was looking for was on neither of those. I didn't know whether to be worried or relieved. If he had somehow slipped through the net, then the authorities would not be making inquiries about him or his family. On the other hand, as a wealthy member of that community he should be listed and it would be anomalous if he were not, and I worried about the possible reasons for that. Anyway, there was no point in speculating about any of that since there were three more lists I hadn't yet seen.

By now people were talking in a very guarded and cautious manner and only to those they believed could be trusted, about the arrests and unexplained disappearances which were becoming more and more frequent. It had become common to pass shops that had closed down or offices where the nameplate had been removed from the entrance.

The wireless was now issuing frequent warnings and exhortations: *Be vigilant! If you are aware of breaches of the hygiene rules, alert your local police.*

* * *

The fact that I had started coming home late was having a bad effect on my wife's nerves. I sympathised. She was dealing on her own with two quarrelsome children and a moody and insolent teenager. I was not being paid extra money for my longer hours, and that annoyed her since, as she pointed out, prices were rising rapidly and my wages had remained stable.

It was a week after the new regime of late working had begun that we had our worst quarrel for many months. We were in our bedroom, and I hoped the girls couldn't hear us. It started with money. She talked of dismissing the servant, and I said I didn't want her to have to do all the work herself.

She snapped: *You leave us no choice. It's that damned girl of yours. Do you know how much she's costing us?*

I said: *I'm keeping a schedule of expenses and when her father gets back he'll reimburse me.*

She screamed: *You've been saying that for months and he hasn't come back yet. Do you think he's ever going to? And if he does, why should he repay us? You know how tight-fisted those people are. And you've heard the girl talk about him. Does he sound like an honourable man?*

I was shocked because she rarely voiced such ignorant preju-dices. I made the mistake of pointing out that we were better off than most people because, since we owned the apartment, we didn't have to pay either rent or a mortgage.

She almost shouted: *That's no credit to you. I inherited it from my father. It wasn't your hard work that earned it. It was my grandfather's.* Then she said: *You made the decision to take in that little nuisance de-spite my objections, and you're making your family suffer.*

I said something I instantly regretted: *If you felt like that, you should have made it clear from the start. I gave you every opportunity to object. I knew we couldn't take the risk of making you ill again.*

Oh, it's my fault, now is it? For doing what you wanted. For having had a breakdown.

No, I didn't mean to say that.

She said: *You're saying you didn't insist on taking her in because you've got some sort of fantasy in your head about her?*

I didn't quite know what she meant, and I didn't want to find out.

* * *

My wife would have been even angrier if I had shared with her a concern that was beginning to trouble me. It had occurred to me as a possibility that the reason why the father was not on the lists I had so far succeeded in scrutinising was that he was not, in fact, wealthy. Did he really own or part-own the department store? Could it be that he was not really as rich as he pretended, and was that the reason why he had sent his daughter to a free school rather than a fee-paying one? On the other hand, if he were hard up, he would surely not have left the house unused and with a staff for so long.

I decided to make another attempt to find out from someone at the store what the situation was.

* * *

So after work the next day I went there and insisted on speaking to someone higher up than the deputy manager I had previously met. Eventually I found myself in the presence of a thuggish man who was rude and dismissive. I could not give him a persuasive reason for asking my questions and so I learned nothing about the girl's father: his relation to the store, his present financial situation, or his whereabouts.

* * *

Now my wife raised with me yet again the idea that we should find a way of getting the girl off our hands. She was convinced the intruder was creating severe disharmony, and I could only agree with her. The way a family evolves is very organic, and to introduce a new element so abruptly was dangerous.

* * *

The question of why the girl's family had not sent word about when they would return was increasingly on my mind. And I discovered it was worrying the girl as well, though I had thought she was unconcerned about it. At the very least I was hoping her brother would be released from whatever prisoner-of-war camp he might be in and would return to take responsibility for his sister—unreliable though he sounded.

At breakfast a day or two later, the girl suddenly demanded she be allowed to go back to her parents' house in order to pick up various articles of dress and pieces of jewellery that she now needed since her absence had become prolonged. I resisted because I had a feeling it might be unwise for her to be seen there. She then changed tack and said she was 'terribly worried' about her family and when they would be back and wanted to find out if any of them had telephoned or written. I wondered which was the real reason. I caught my wife's eye in case, like myself, she was afraid the girl might have heard some of the rumours that were being circulated.

Although I assured her that I called in every week and was going to do so again in a few days, that failed to satisfy her. She suddenly blurted out: *Do you think my parents and my brothers will be back in time for my birthday?*

That was two months away, and my wife and I hastened to assure her they would be. But I was beginning to wonder. Her brother might be a prisoner-of-war for very much longer.

I continued to resist letting her go back to the house because I was concerned she might reveal something to the servant that could lead the authorities to take an interest in me. For I now looked back with relief on the misunderstanding that meant the woman did not know who I was or where I lived. I was certain she would report to the authorities anything that might earn her a reward—especially if it harmed the girl and her family.

And yet, by the same token, it meant that if the child's father and mother had indeed written or telephoned, the servant would not be able to tell them where she was. That was unsatisfactory for a number of reasons. Reflecting that it would be expedient for the woman to be able to tell the parents she had recently seen the child, I agreed she should accompany me when I made my weekly visit next Tuesday.

I discussed with my wife whether to tell the girl she must say nothing that revealed to anyone who we were or where we lived. My wife was surprised I was concerned about that, and I found it hard to explain my motive. I just had a feeling it might be a wise precaution. In the end I decided to say nothing to the girl, since there was no advantage in worrying her.

During this conversation my wife said: *While you're at the house you can try out the idea of her going back to live there and see how it goes down with both of them.*

I had to agree to that.

* * *

On Tuesday afternoon after work I met the girl, who was carrying a large empty suitcase given her by my wife, at a tram-stop near her house as we had arranged. When I rang the bell the servant opened the door. She did not look at all pleased to see us and glanced at the suitcase with unconcealed dismay. It came to me suddenly that she had been hoping never to see the girl again and was now afraid she was moving back.

When the girl asked her—as she did in crossing the threshold—if there had been any news from her parents, the woman replied vaguely and evasively.

The girl persisted, and as she spoke she was tearing open the letters to her father and mother that had been piled up on the hall-table, throwing each aside when she found it had nothing to do with the whereabouts of her family. I noticed that many of them were demands for money, and I wondered about the bills that were not being paid for items like gas and telephone. At last the servant admitted that a message had come from the girl's parents to say they would be delayed longer than they had expected. Of course the girl fired a series of questions at her: Who did you speak to? Was it

Mama? How did she sound? Was Father with her? How is my little brother? Is there any news of my elder brother?

Everything had to be extracted as laboriously as if teeth were being drawn. As far as we could establish, someone other than the parents had telephoned the house a few days earlier. The servant apparently had no idea who was speaking—or she was concealing their identity—but the caller had said that the girl's parents were still in the Western Zone and would be delaying their return because they had been invited to a place in the country nearby.

The girl looked relieved but puzzled and said she did not know what friends of her parents lived near the former capital.

I found myself wondering if the woman was saying anything at all that was true. Had someone telephoned? If so, had that been the message? The fact that she had been so reluctant to mention that there had been a communication at all from the girl's parents made me suspicious. The reference to their being delayed was odd since the border between the two zones was still closed to all but a few individuals who had enough influence with the occupying power to be allowed across or were able to pay bribes. Was 'delayed' a euphemism for 'unable to cross the border'?

The girl seized the suitcase from me and ran up the stairs. I saw a look of relief on the woman's face as she realised it was empty and we had come to fill it, and she volunteered that she supposed the girl would stay on with me until further developments. I said that remained to be decided and it was possible the girl might move back, and she made no attempt to conceal her dismay.

A few minutes later the girl came running down the stairs shouting that the servant was a thief. She was almost hysterical, spitting abuse at the woman, who glared back at her. When I was able to get from her what the fuss was about, she told me that an attempt had been made to break into the safe in her parents' bedroom. She dragged me up the stairs and into the room and showed me a coffer which was set into the wall and usually concealed by a picture that she had swung to one side. There were signs around its edges that someone had used something like a crowbar to try—unsuccessfully—to open it and, failing that, to force it out of the wall.

The servant had followed us up. She stood there, stupidly saying she knew nothing about it and someone must have got into the house while she was out shopping. The girl accused her in the crudest terms of having done it herself.

I told the woman to leave the room and then asked the girl if she knew the combination so we could take the safe's contents with us. Unfortunately, she did not. It was a model I was familiar with from the office, and I knew it was virtually impregnable. She wanted us to go straight to the nearest police-station and report the servant for attempted theft and have her arrested or at least evicted from the house. I knew it was advisable to have as little as possible to do with the authorities, and told her I would not permit her to do that. She was furious with me. I now saw yet again what a little minx she could be when she did not get her way.

We found the woman downstairs. She had heard the girl shouting at me about the police, and she could see that I understood what a weak position we were in.

The two of them started screaming at each other, and the girl used words I could not have imagined she knew. She shouted that she was not going to leave the house while 'that woman' was there because she was planning to steal everything in it. At last I managed to drag her away and calm her down in one of the other rooms. I told her she should fill the suitcase with as many valuables as she could, and I promised to return to the house at regular and more frequent intervals to make sure no further attempt had been made to remove or break into the safe. She took a great deal of persuading, but at last she agreed.

She began to go round the house gathering up things, and now she found that a precious piece of porcelain had disappeared. She flung herself into a chair and sobbed: *Mummy loved that vase.*

I challenged the woman, and she said she had not been paid for many months. She had sold 'one or two things', just to cover her wages and pay a few utilities bills. I told her that if the girl had described it accurately and she had received a fair price, that single object should have covered her wages and all the bills for several years.

While I was talking to her, the girl discovered other acts of theft and kept running back to tell me that such and such an ornament or picture had disappeared. Plenty of precious artefacts remained, however, and I told her to make an inventory of those that we were going to have to leave behind. She did so, and it took a couple of hours. At last we had packed the suitcase until it was so full that it was hard to close, and we were ready to leave.

I warned the woman I would be back soon and reminded her that I now had an inventory of *objets d'art* and that if anything else disappeared, I would go to the police. She stared boldly back at me, as if silently defying me to do that. I didn't raise again the possibility of the girl's coming back because it was clearly out of the question now.

I carried the suitcase down the stairs and as I approached the front-door, just by chance my gaze fell on a shelf in the hall which was too high for the girl to have seen. There was a telegram lying on it. I picked it up and found it was addressed simply with the name of the family and the street. It was unopened. I handed it to the girl. She ripped it open and gasped, and I took it from her. In six words it stated that her brother was in a certain prisoner-of-war camp.

I had assumed she had little affection for him from the way she had spoken of him, so I was surprised that she seemed so shocked.

I told her this was excellent news: he was alive, and they had not said he was injured. She looked doubtful but then accepted that.

I looked at the woman. She did not even look embarrassed. She said she had put the telegram there for safe keeping and had forgotten about it.

The date was more than two weeks earlier, which meant she had neglected to mention it to me on my previous visit as well.

* * *

Afterwards I thought about the servant's negligence over the message and the telegram. It horrified me that the woman should care
so little for what the girl was suffering, even if she had reasons for
disliking her.

Also I could not help thinking about the safe. On the way
home I had asked the girl what was in it. She said it was where
her mother's jewellery was kept and then, unprompted, gave me a
lengthy and detailed description of it which made clear that it was
of considerable value. Moreover, she had once happened to go into
that room while her father was opening the safe. Apart from the
jewels she had noticed a wad of banknotes, some small bars of gold,
and various documents which sounded to me like bonds. I hoped
nothing would happen to the safe, and it seemed so wrong that its
contents should fall into the hands of thieves.

Something else occurred to me later that evening. Thinking
back over the servant's words, it struck me that she said she had not
been paid 'for many months', and I wondered if she meant her salary had fallen into arrears even before her employer had gone away.

* * *

Things were moving forward at work. I was given a revised list that
now contained the names of thirty wealthy men from the girl's community in the city. Her father's name was still not there. I was struck
by the fact that against each name there was one of two rubrics. In
most cases it read: *The subject's property is now under the guardianship of the Department of Protection.* In a few instances, however, the
wording was: *The subject has been relocated and the property restored to
the ownership of the nation.*

I wondered what the difference was.

* * *

That Sunday a reduction in the salaries of all public servants was
announced on the evening news. It was a cut of twenty percent, and

it was to take immediate effect. From the beginning of that week I would be earning one-fifth less. Coupled with the steep increase in prices since the invasion, I calculated that my income from that point was going to be not much more than two-thirds what it had been before the War in terms of what it could buy. And because of the girl's presence, our domestic expenses had increased by about one-seventh. I said nothing to the girls, but later that night I talked it over with my wife.

We realised we had to make drastic savings.

From now on, we would eat only the cheapest cuts of meat, bank down the heating from the stove, and economise on baths and hot water. The major item about which we had to make a decision was, of course, the domestic. But an easy decision was to reduce the pocket-money we gave the three girls. The eldest was still looking for work and so needed enough to cover tram-fares and snacks. Beyond that, we could give her almost nothing for little luxuries and treats. The same was true of our younger daughter, who needed her school-money to pay for fares and occasional bars of chocolate. The girl, however, had no need for pocket-money since she never left the apartment alone and we gave her everything.

We decided to tell them at supper the next day. It started well. My elder daughter said she understood and that she had just heard of what might be an opening for part-time work. It would be badly paid but would at least allow her to learn her craft from a good dressmaker. My younger daughter also accepted it with philosoph-ical resignation. The girl, however, made a fuss. She asked why she could not be given the same amount as my younger daughter less the tram-fares? I patiently explained she had no need for money. I pointed out that it was entirely reasonable for my younger daugh-ter to have to buy an occasional snack on her way to or back from school.

The girl remained unpersuaded and seemed determined to be-lieve I was discriminating against her. Then she suddenly stood up and said: *You don't like me, do you?* To our astonishment she turned and ran out of the room.

When the door slammed behind her my younger girl said: *No, we don't like you.*

We all sat in silence for a moment avoiding each other's glance. Then I pointed out how difficult it was for the girl to be amongst strangers and worrying about her own family, and said we must make allowances.

My elder daughter became very quiet after that, and when her sister had gone to bed, said she wanted to talk to us seriously. Once the three of us were alone, she said: *We're all suffering now because of the girl. She must be costing us a considerable amount. It's not fair to make me and my sister pay for her. And it's not just the money.*

I said: *Looking after her might lead to my getting a much better job. You know that. You're being selfish.*

She said: *You're the one who's being selfish. You know there isn't much chance of that happening. You're just indulging a whim at our expense.*

She said it without knowing, of course, that I was already wondering just how wealthy the girl's father was. I found I couldn't answer her.

I said: *You're nearly eighteen. If it weren't for the Occupation you would be earning your own living by now, and you'd be contributing to household expenses for your subsistence in lieu of a share of rent. But we're letting you live here and feeding you for nothing.*

She flared up at that and said: *You've no right to speak of rent.*

I said: *I just meant that if you couldn't live here, you would have to share an apartment with other girls and pay rent.*

She said: *You know I couldn't afford to do that even if I could find a job. It's not fair of you to talk like that. You two don't pay rent and neither should I. This apartment belongs to my sister and me as much as it does to you. You both inherited it and you have an obligation to pass it on. It's not yours to do with as you please.*

I was puzzled that she had made that point and I asked: *What do you mean?*

She said: *Letting a complete stranger move in. I want my nice room back.*

I made it clear that there could be no question of that, and she stalked off in a rage.

My wife had said very little during the argument, but as soon as we were alone she made it clear she believed our daughter was justified in her assertion that I was sacrificing the interests of my family for the sake of the 'intruder'.

When she reproached me—as she did now—for my failure to earn enough to give the family what she wanted for them, I was reluctant to defend myself. I could never let myself forget that our dire financial state—even before the War and the girl—was due to my having failed my final qualifying examinations. I couldn't blame my wife for having been so unwell at the time. Her passionate desire for some years had been, in spite of the apartment having been in her family for decades, that we move to a larger one in a better part of the city since the district had gone so rapidly downhill. It was clear that was impossible.

I didn't manage to get much sleep that night. My relations with my elder child had been difficult for a long time. There were aspects of her personality that disappointed me. I suppose you can love someone without much liking them. I was particularly upset that she had chosen to say those things in front of her mother, whose nervous condition she had only too good a reason to know about. I would have to speak to her about that.

* * *

After the discussion of pocket-money, the girl sulked all the next day and—as my wife told me when I got home—scarcely emerged from the room that she had to herself while my younger child was at school. My elder daughter similarly stayed in her room, and the two ate at different times to avoid meeting.

When our younger girl had got back from school she told my wife that she and the girl were not speaking to each other— which was awkward when they were sharing not just a room but the bed.

My wife led me into our room and shut the door. She told me the situation was becoming intolerable. It was up to me to exercise my authority. I promised to discuss it with our elder child that evening.

So after supper I summoned her into my study. I promised her I was going to take steps to rectify the situation with our unwanted guest and insisted that in the meantime, she must not make things more difficult for her mother. I said: *You must agree to certain conditions. Don't pick a quarrel with your mother and don't even quarrel with me in her presence. If anything is worrying you, discuss it with me when we're alone. You know why I'm saying this.*

My daughter said: *You're talking to the wrong person. It's Mother who let me down. She's always preferred my sister and never made any secret of it.*

I couldn't deny the truth of that. I just said: *You're old enough now to understand that your mother was seriously unwell at various times early in your life. These things happen and they're nobody's fault but they can inhibit the normal mother-child relationship from developing. Your mother has tried to have a good relationship with you and it's up to you to play your part.*

My wife and I had an argument that night when the girls were all in bed. My wife brought up all the things that had happened since the girl's arrival and said she was destroying our family. I tried to persuade her that the girl's father might return and give me a job, but I knew I was not being convincing because I had realised by now how unlikely that was. I didn't use the argument again that the servant at the house was not someone to be trusted with a child.

Eventually we agreed to tell the girl that we had decided she should go back to her family's house. My wife would say nothing to her the next day until I returned from work. But she would tell our elder child immediately what we had decided.

* * *

When I got home I found that my elder daughter was more cheerful than she had been for many weeks.

After supper I said there was something we needed to discuss—all of us. We sat at the table and I said to the girl: *My wife and I feel that it's better for you if you go back to your own house.*

She stared at me as if I had struck her. Such a wounded, unhappy look.

She said: *But you're my new mummy and daddy. These are my sisters now. I've always wanted a sister and now I've got two.*

I said: *That's a very charming thing to say but the truth is, we're not your family. We think it would be better for you to be in your own home now.*

Her face began to crumple and she wailed: *Please don't make me go back there. She's so horrible to me. You know she's been stealing. She doesn't want me there.*

My younger daughter was now in tears. I saw that my wife was moved as well. I think it was the idea that the girl saw her as a second mother that had touched her.

My wife caught my eye and seeing that she was as upset as I, I said: *Leave us for a moment, all of you.*

The three girls went out.

When the door had closed behind them I said: *We can't throw her out. It's just not right.*

My wife said: *What do you suggest?*

She's right about that servant, I said. *She shouldn't be left alone with her. We'll have to let her stay a little longer.*

She said: *Until when? What about until the first school she can go to opens? It must be soon.*

Knowing what I did, I was doubtful such schools would ever be opened. However, we agreed that as soon as schools for children of the girl's kind were opened, we would hand her over to her own people and let them look after her. If necessary we would tell the school authorities she was their responsibility, and our home was no longer open to her.

We called the girls back in and told them what we had decided. The two younger ones hugged each other and then each of us.

The next afternoon while the domestic was in the apartment, I went into the kitchen and found the girl in tears being hugged by her. I assumed the girl had told her she would be leaving fairly soon.

My elder daughter made no attempt to hide the fact that she was furious. She marched me into the study and said it was intolerable that her mother and I had gone back on our promise. She said: *You've given her* carte blanche *to stay forever.*

I denied it, but I believed she was probably right. I felt sorry for what my wife and I had decided. And I began to notice from about this point that my wife now rarely smiled at the girl and spoke to her less than in the past. Her feelings towards her had become increasingly negative, and she was starting to wind down what relationship they had had in order to prepare herself for its imminent and complete severance. Though I understood and even sympathised with that, I also resented it. I felt she was loading the burden of guilt and the pain of our loss of the girl—for there would be regret as well as relief—entirely onto me.

* * *

What was happening at home was not my only worry. Conditions at work were becoming worse. On the Monday of that week, the deadline had arrived by which wealthy men in the 'protected community' should have declared their assets. The director—who, in contrast to the head and the deputy-head of my section, I had always believed to be a decent man—called us together and announced that the first phase was complete. Now we were entering the second, which involved double-checking what we had learned and trying to find assets that had been concealed. He said: *We've asked the wealthy to come forward but I fear that some of them will instead have tried to conceal their assets.*

We would address this in two ways. He explained that half of us would now make an inventory of all the property—real and personal—above a certain value thought to belong to anyone in the 'protected community'. This would be done secretly. As he put it: *We'll catch any defaulters by working from the other direction: start with the assets and find the owner.*

The other half of his staff would be interrogating men on the list to find out if they had tried to hide assets. By the end of this phase we would have identified the assets of the wealthy members of the 'protected community' either listed by themselves or detected if they had failed to report them. Once we had identified assets belonging to a specific individual, we would freeze them and they would be seized. He ended by saying that our heads of section would allocate specific duties. I was hoping I would be assigned to trace assets since that might allow me, with luck, to investigate the ownership of the store.

My head of section immediately called us—me and the seven colleagues at my level—into his office where he was waiting with his deputy. He said: *Enough of all this list-making. Now we're going to start putting the screws on the bastards.* Then he looked at me and added: *If that's all right with you.*

I tried to smile as if he were making a joke, but I knew he realised how little I liked this work. It was for that reason, I believe, that by deliberate malice, when he divided us into two groups, he assigned me to interrogate men on the list. He knew how much I would hate that task.

The four of us were each given a numbered list and the head and his deputy also had one each. Each individual on the list would be summoned for examination. The head of section required that when each person was interviewed about the return he had lodged, we should assume he had lied about his assets. He said: *We all know from experience how devious and greedy these people are and we need to take measures in the light of that. The relatives and friends will know pretty much what the assets of any individual actually are and so what we'll do is to bring pressure on the one in front of us and force him to reveal the true assets of, say, his brother-in-law or his business partner.*

So that he could show us how it was done, we had to sit in on the first few of his interviews. He shook the Return of Assets in the face of his victim and bellowed that he knew he was lying. That went on for some minutes while the poor man sat white-faced in silence. Then in a more reasonable tone the head would say: *We will seize all your assets if you don't tell us what your sister's husband owns.*

I tried to conceal how appalled I was by this. I have always believed that if there are no laws and there is only arbitrary power then nothing has meaning or value, and I don't want to live in a world like that. However, I had no choice but to go through the motions at the very least.

The richest hundred and fifty families were divided among the four senior people in our section: the head, his deputy, my friendly colleague, and myself. Of course the first thing I did was to scan my list to see if the girl's father was on it. He was not. It was then easy enough for me to find an opportunity when my colleague was out of the room to look at his. The name was not there either.

There were strict rules about keeping files locked up and away from the sight of anyone who had no legitimate reason for seeing them, and therefore it would be hard to get a sight of the lists being processed by my two superiors.

The returns began to arrive, and we spent some time confirming what we had been told and trying to find out if anything had been hidden. That involved talking to the bank-managers and accountants of the subjects and often to their employees. Then we summoned the men on 'our' list and interviewed them. My colleague and I did this in the room we shared. I hated having to shout at and intimidate them, and I freely admit that I was not very good at it. On the other hand, I was saddened to see how willingly and effectively my colleague—the one man at work apart from the director whom I had regarded as a decent person—went about these unsavoury tasks.

Now that I was spending so much of my time encouraging informers and tracking down assets using these methods, I knew how meticulous the search was both for property and for people themselves belonging to that section of society. And of course it was especially the wealthy ones who were being put under scrutiny.

I went over and over in my mind what the authorities knew about the girl's family to try to work out how probable it was that they would take an interest in them and in her. It was virtually certain that the family would come within their purview through their ownership of the store. What I did not know was if the girl's father was the sole proprietor or if he had one or more partners. (Assuming he was involved in its ownership at all!) If the latter, then if an official summoned one of the co-owners for interrogation, it was likely that the issue of his partner would arise.

I asked the girl about her father's involvement in the store, but she was irritatingly unenlightening—presumably because she did not know anything about her father's business and had probably never thought about the matter.

It was one afternoon about now that I casually asked my head of section what the difference in meaning was between the two rubrics on the list of names. Without looking up, he just said: *Once the subject has been relocated, then, obviously, the assets default directly to the state.*

* * *

Amid the growing gloom, something hopeful happened at last. The next day my elder daughter came home and announced with some satisfaction that she had found work. It was very poorly paid and in a distant part of the city, so her tram-fare would reduce her earnings still further. But she would be able to make a small contribution to the household expenses. Later my wife told me that the job was only temporary to see if she 'suited'. The establishment was not one that had a wealthy or remotely fashionable clientèle, although the quality of their work was good. At least it meant she would not be associating with collaborationists.

That evening I opened one of our remaining bottles of wine to celebrate.

From now on my elder daughter left the house with her sister
and myself and caught the same tram as her sibling.

* * *

I was now so busy that for several weeks I had had no time to visit
the house on Tuesdays as I had promised the girl I would. She pes-
tered me about that every evening when I got home—exhausted as
I was. She knew from the wireless about the regulation requiring
a return of assets and was anxious that I should take the inventory
of all the valuables her parents owned and register it with my own
department. She believed that was the only means of preventing
their being stolen by the servant.

I tried to explain to her that was wholly inappropriate as well as
impossible. I avoided telling her it would be unwise to draw attention to her father and herself, but I told her that her father's assets
were not my concern. Though I did not say it, I thought that such a
preoccupation with wealth was unnatural and unhealthy in a child
of that age.

* * *

My daughter's small subventions would not materially improve our
financial situation and so the day after she found work, my wife and
I took a decision about the domestic. My wife was pretty sure that
she was no longer stealing from us, if she ever had been—and that
was perhaps because money was tighter and so she had less latitude.

There was a difficulty. We were worried that if we let her go, she
might make use of her knowledge of the girl's presence to avenge
herself on us. We agreed to try to dismiss her the next day but to
tread carefully, as if edging over the thin ice on a frozen lake. If she
even hinted that she would make trouble, we would withdraw and
keep her on, telling her she had misunderstood our meaning.

* * *

In the office we began to draw up accounts for our 'clients' as we smilingly called the wealthy individuals whose holdings we were investigating. We subordinates were instructed to report to the head and his deputy whenever we discovered the existence of a safe or a bank-deposit. They would then deal with it themselves on the grounds that we were not to be trusted. The two of them would each be a witness for the probity of the other.

I noticed they were not very interested in real property even though that was where the highest values were.

* * *

As arranged, I came home from work early enough to catch the domestic while she was still there. She looked surprised to see me, and I think she guessed what was coming. My wife set the girl a task in the living-room, and then we three adults sat round the kitchen-table. My wife and I began to talk about the effects of the rise in prices. Some things had doubled—or even tripled—while my salary had dropped by a fifth. She must have guessed what we were leading towards because she started talking about how difficult things were for her with her husband being too unwell to work and a daughter still at school.

Since she had not hinted that she could make trouble for us over the girl, we went on to say we were terribly sorry but we just could not afford her services any more. She looked shocked and asked if she could work just three days a week or even two. (We had talked this over and agreed that if we were going to dismiss her, it had to be a clean break. To have her coming to the house but being resentful at being given half the work was the worst of all options.) We told her we could not afford to have her even for one day. She was silent for a moment and then said: *You can afford to take in this girl and feed her and she isn't even your own kind.*

My wife and I looked at each other? Was this a hint that she knew she could make things awkward for us? What did she mean by *your own kind*? Did she merely mean that the girl was not a blood-relative in which case the remark was perfectly harmless. Or was she alluding to the girl's membership of a different community and warning us that she could get us into trouble? I thought not and so I said: *I'm very sorry but that's what we've decided. We won't need you to come again.*

She got up and slowly took off her apron and then put on her coat. She went to the door and just said: *I'll miss the children.*

My wife said: *And they'll miss you. We all will.*

It was the truth. She was a cheerful soul.

We went and told the girl that the domestic was leaving and would not be coming back. There was an emotional parting between the two of them. My younger daughter arrived from school in time to join in and shed a few tears. Rather to my dismay, the girl said: *Come and visit us. Promise.*

It was odd that the girl was so aware of her superior wealth and sophisticated life in comparison with my family and lost no opportunity to lord it over my daughters, and yet at the same time she had no reserve or self-consciousness with folk like the domestic or the joiner's wife. I suppose she did not see them as people to whom she had to prove her superiority. Or perhaps it was because she felt she could give them orders.

The girl was so upset afterwards that she turned on my wife and myself and said: *I suppose you sacked her because she stole a few things.*

So I was right and she had known that. I wondered if she had been blackmailing the woman. Yet in that case they would surely not have been on such good terms.

Seeing our surprise, she said: *Oh I know all about what she was getting up to. How she fiddled the change from the money for shopping and so on. But her husband is an invalid and she can hardly feed her family. I don't know how they'll manage now. It's not fair you did that to her.*

I said I was surprised that she was so sorry to see the domestic go since it was she who had damaged her doll. She just looked at me with contempt and flounced out of the room.

I said to my wife: *She seems so sure that the domestic wasn't responsible for the doll that I think there can be only one explanation: She did it herself.*

My wife looked at me strangely but made no reply. I began to wonder if she had learned or guessed more of the truth about that incident than she was prepared to tell me.

* * *

The bureaucracy imposed on us by the occupying power was simultaneously meticulous in its attention to detail and blundering in its overall strategy. An example of that was what now happened at work. My section had been processing the returns of assets for several weeks when it was realised that there was no way to ensure compliance by the 'protected community' with the requirement to register their possessions when the authorities had no knowledge of who was and who was not a member of that community. They could not carry out random checks when they had no list of who was subject to the regulation. This problem had emerged across the country.

And so the day after we had parted from the domestic, the Ministry of Protection announced a new regulation. All members of the 'protected community' over the age of fourteen had to go to their local Department of Protection and register their addresses 'for their own security' and must not move house without reporting their new address to the department within a week of the move. On registering they would be given a new and distinctive identity-card in exchange for the existing one. Those under that age could be registered by their parents now but were not required to, although they would have to be registered by a later unspecified date. The deadline for registration of those over fourteen was two months in the future.

My wife and I were relieved that the girl was outside the scope of those regulations because she was not yet fourteen—though her birthday was only a few weeks away. I was pleased I did not have to make a decision about whether or not she should register. She was clearly in an anomalous position, so there was ambiguity about her status. My wife agreed that we should wait for her parents to return and leave it to them to sort it out. After all, we said to each other, if we registered the girl now, we would not know which was the correct address to give for her—our own or that of her parents.

* * *

That week-end things came to a head inside the apartment. For weeks tensions had been building up. The various privations—the bad food, the cold because we could not afford to heat the apartment as before, the power-cuts that were becoming more frequent and meant we sometimes spent the evening in darkness unable to read and without the comfort of the wireless—were making us all tired and less willing to put up with each other's irritating habits.

My wife had stopped buying special foodstuffs to accommodate the girl—we simply could not afford to. Rationing had been announced, though not yet introduced, but prices had risen steeply. That was a form of rationing by cost which made certain items unaffordable, and, given how short of cash we were, my wife and I had little patience for the girl's faddishness about food. She refused to eat bacon or pork or pig's trotters, and often those were all that was on sale at the butcher's. In protest, she simply left the food uneaten on her plate and one of our daughters would take it.

My elder daughter would come home exhausted after a hard day at work followed by a long tram-ride. Her new employer had shown herself to be a difficult person to work for and was constantly making new and unreasonable demands: tidy the work-room, clean the shop, make lunch for the other seamstresses. My daughter felt that she was being treated like a skivvy rather than an apprentice whose low wages reflected the fact that she was there to learn as much as to work.

She complained that on the few occasions her employer had allowed her to do anything creative, she had been dismissive of her designs, and she believed it was because she was an embittered old woman who was envious of her youth and talent. What made it worse was that the couturière had a favourite, a girl of about the same age who had also only just been taken on as an apprentice. She gave her far more interesting work to do, and she had already begun to help with the design of the dresses. My daughter remarked that she suspected that the woman was a member of the girl's community and this explained why she was so spiteful and penny-pinching.

A new problem arose. My elder daughter began to demand a bigger role in decisions about the way we lived and when I objected, she pointed out that the household now had two wage-earners, and I had to concede the point—though in truth her contribution was very small. It irked her more than ever that we were making heavy sacrifices for the girl, and on several occasions, when she was alone with my wife and myself, she revealed her unhappiness that some of her cash was going towards feeding 'the ingrate'.

In fact, we were all becoming less indulgent towards the girl's boastfulness and querulousness. And then on that Sunday evening there was an incident at supper that marked what turned out to be the beginning of a new stage in the deterioration of our relations with her.

She had been chattering on as usual about the amusing things she and her friends used to get up to. I wasn't paying any attention, and I didn't think anyone else was, but suddenly my younger girl said indignantly: *The other day you said your best friend's parents have a house by the lake and now you're saying it's halfway up a mountain!*

The girl's face shut down as if a steel gate had descended and her expression was as hard as an old woman's. She pushed her chair back and said: *You're stupid. You weren't listening properly. I'm not going to talk to you any more.*

Then she stood up and made for the door. My wife called out to her to come back since she had not been given permission to leave the table, but she ignored her and went out. We heard the slamming of the door of the bedroom.

My elder daughter said: *How long is this going to go on? How long am I going to be deprived of my own bedroom?*

It was not so much a question as a statement of suffering, and nobody responded to it.

The girl did not reappear until very late that evening. The rest of us were sitting in the living-room reading a book or listening to the concert on the wireless when she quietly came in and sat down. In a perfectly calm voice she said to my younger daughter: *It was wrong of you to say that, but I forgive you. You became confused about what I said. My friend's family sold one house—the one by the lake— and bought a different one.*

It was said with great dignity. My younger daughter responded well. She said: *I'm sorry if I offended you. I didn't mean to.*

That, however, was not to be the end of the matter—not by a long way.

* * *

The next morning as I was walking with my daughters towards the tram-stop, my younger girl brought up the incident and said: *I think she realised she had been caught lying and she went off and thought up that explanation. But I remembered later that she said she had visited the house on the mountain two summers ago and the one by the lake only last summer.*

I said: *It doesn't matter if she is making things up. Remember, she's missing her family. She's trying to live in her happiest moments and they're all in the past.*

My younger child nodded and seemed to understand what I was saying. But the elder said: *I don't think lying is ever acceptable. You've never allowed us to lie, Father. And she's not just lying for her own sake. She's doing it to make us feel dowdy and boring in comparison with her.*

I said: *She doesn't need to lie. Her father is very rich and there's nothing false about that.*

Strangely enough, as soon as I had uttered those words my doubts about that claim were reinforced. I had assumed the man was wealthy because he appeared to own—or part-own—the big store and because he lived in a handsome house and had bought valuable possessions. But as an accountant I had learned that the appearance of wealth did not always mean that it existed. I recalled the demands for money I had seen the girl dropping on the floor at the house and wondered if some of them were for more than things like gas and telephone. And, of course, there was the anomaly that his name had not appeared on any of the lists of wealthy men that I had managed to get sight of.

When I talked about it to my wife that evening, she said she believed that what the girl was exaggerating was not the wealth of her family and their circle, but the richness of her own social life. That struck me as likely to be the truth. In that case it wasn't the country villa she was inventing but the best friend. So was it that the girl was too quarrelsome to be invited to the houses of her father's business associates, or was it that the family itself was being ostracised by the rest of the community?

What was the truth about the thuggish man I had spoken to at the store? Was the girl's father disliked because he employed bullies like that? Or did that man represent a faction that had seized control of the store?

* * *

When my younger daughter arrived home from school that afternoon, she found that the vanity carousel had been partly dismantled and placed under the girls' bed. My wife described to me later the argument between the two children that had then taken place. My daughter asked the girl why she had done that, and she replied that it had only been given on loan and she had decided she wanted it back. My daughter pointed out that she clearly had no intention of using it since she had put it away, but the girl said she wanted to stop it suffering wear and tear from my daughter's use.

My daughter had said: *I don't care. I didn't like the horrible thing anyway. Father says it's stupid to care so much about your appearance. He says only someone with nothing in their head cares about things like that.*

This enraged the girl, and my wife had to intervene physically to part them.

That evening my elder daughter said to my wife and myself that she was not prepared to go on sleeping for much longer in what she called 'a child's bed in a child's room'.

* * *

I'm sure I wasn't the only person in our section who was surprised by how rarely the head and his deputy found anything of value when emptying the safes and bank-deposit boxes.

The safest strategy was to ignore what was obviously going on. Then one day it became impossible for me to remain uninvolved. One of my 'clients', a wealthy lawyer, pointed out that certain assets had been in his bank-deposit-box and yet they had apparently not been found there by the head of section. He was worried he would be accused of having concealed them. That situation had arisen before, and the 'client' had simply been charged with having hidden whatever was missing. What created the difficulty in this case was that the witness had made a 'certified deposit' in which the manager of the bank had witnessed the action and had retained the key.

I wondered what to do. The correct procedure in normal circumstances would have been to report those facts to the director. However, these were not normal circumstances. Yet if I did not protect myself, I might be accused of taking part in the thefts that were being carried out.

I decided to ask my friendly colleague. He agreed with me that going to the director would be ill-advised. I could not be sure I would be protected from the vengeance of my head and his deputy. To my astonishment, however, he suggested I should hint to our head of section that I knew what he was doing and would make trouble unless I was paid a share of the proceeds. Such a course of action would be not merely corrupt but crazy. My head of section was a cunning and ruthless man and to cross him in that way would be foolhardy.

I decided to close my eyes to what I had learned. I had already written in my report: *The individual claims that the assets listed above should have been found in his box.* Now I tore that up and rewrote it without that sentence. I had problems enough without looking for new ones.

* * *

The girl was becoming more of a problem every day. Now that the domestic was not in the apartment for several hours and able to soak up her attention, my wife told me that she trailed listlessly after her from room to room most of the day. When she was bored she fiddled with things and often broke them: the knob from the wireless, the switch on one of the lamps. For someone so captivated by objects like jewellery and clothes, she had surprisingly little manual intuition. The burden of keeping her entertained and out of mischief now fell fully on my wife. All the respite she had lay in the girl's visits to the apartment below. And then those came to an end.

That Thursday the girl had come hurrying back from the apartment below in tears. She went straight into her bedroom and slammed the door. Had she been caught out telling fibs? Had her boasting finally alienated the good-natured wife of the joiner? Or was it something to do with the old man? She would not tell us. My wife had tapped on the door, but she had refused to emerge for several hours. When she did, she wouldn't say anything about what had happened.

I wondered if the joiner's wife had grown tired of her difficult ways and quarrelled with her. Yet the girl seemed to behave much better with her than with us—just as she had with the domestic. Or perhaps the bigoted old man had realised what her background was and said something to her. Whatever had happened, that was the end of her visits to the apartment, and that meant she was in my wife's hair the whole day.

* * *

After what he had said, I no longer trusted the colleague I had re-garded as a friend. It was frustrating that while I was being required in my professional life to do things that were not only immoral but absurd, there was nobody in the office to whom I dared breathe a hint of criticism of the policies being followed by the authorities. And even my friends outside work would not approach the topic. Rumours of denunciations and arrests were rife, and everyone was terrified of being betrayed.

It occurred to me that in just a few weeks the girl would reach the age of fourteen. If that had happened a few weeks earlier, she would have been required to trade her existing identity-card for one of the new ones and register her address, but since no new an-nouncement had been made about children reaching that age after the date already announced, I assumed that was not the case.

When I got home I went into the living-room and found my two daughters sitting with their heads together over a book of fash-ion-plates. I remembered how often I had seen them playing with each other when they were younger and before the temperamen-tal and academic differences between them had begun to create an estrangement. The girl was in the bedroom, so for a while I could pretend to myself that things were as they had been before the War started and before the intruder had come into our lives. As I kissed them I felt a surge of guilt at having admitted the girl into our world and thereby having done something that had the potential to endanger still further our family's precarious situation.

* * *

Only three days later, the introduction of rationing was announced. Everyone would have to take their identity-card to a new Department of Alimentation where it would be stamped and they would be is-sued with a ration-card. This was dreadful news for us. It meant that five of us were going to have to share the rations intended for four. I just hoped that only the most basic foodstuffs would be affected and it would be possible to buy additional supplies. For a while that was the case. Only bread and other wheaten products, sugar, and dairy foods were rationed. Within a few weeks, however, the scope was extended. And even now prices of food continued to rise.

My wife and I agreed that we would not allow our daughters to give up even the smallest share of their rations. We would feed the girl out of our own allowance. For a while that posed no great problem since we were still able to supplement what the government allowed us by purchase. The fact that the girl was picky about food was at this stage no more than an irritant. Food that she refused to eat was gobbled up by one of the other girls, and that seemed only fair since it had come out of my wife's and my ration.

* * *

The deadline for the registration of all aliens—as they were now called—over the age of fourteen having passed, the local Department of Protection had published an index of names of all those dwelling within the city. There was a copy in my section and I was able to look at it. Nobody was listed under the girl's family name. That meant, I assumed, that her parents had registered as residents in the old capital. I had assumed that someone associated with the department store would register the girl's father even though he was not on the list of wealthy aliens, but that had not happened. Did it mean that he had no involvement with the store? Whatever its implications, it seemed to be a reason to feel relieved. The less likely the family name was to receive attention, the better.

* * *

Now something happened that sounds trivial but which, given the way we were all living on top of each other in circumstances that were daily becoming more straitened, had a significant impact on our little household.

At breakfast the following Monday my elder daughter asked: *Has anyone seen my diamond brooch?* (It was a small and rather expensive ornament that her mother and I had given her for her sixteenth birthday.) She said it accusingly and her gaze lingered on the girl, who seemed perfectly unselfconscious, as if it had not occurred to her that she was under suspicion.

As I was walking my daughters to the tram-stop a little later, the elder told us she was convinced that the girl had stolen it. She said she had once shown it to her, and she had been very taken by it. I pointed out that the girl had several pieces of jewellery of her own that were more valuable, and I could see no reason for her to have stolen it. My elder child said: *It's not the value, Father. She's taken it to hurt me.* I asked her to do nothing about it since she had no proof. But she insisted she had left the brooch in the bathroom and the girl had gone in after her. An hour or so later she had realised it was missing and had looked in the place where she had put it but failed to find it. She said she was sure the girl had locked it in the cherrywood box she had brought with her and which nobody had ever seen opened after her first day in the apartment.

I forgot about the incident, but the next day it happened that I got home earlier than usual while my wife was still out shopping with the girl. My elder child was already there, but the younger had not got back from school. Suddenly my daughter came into the sitting-room triumphantly brandishing a book. It was an adventure story for children. Looking through it, she said, it was clear that the girl had been borrowing from it for her accounts of her social life. It was all there: the picnics, sailing on the lake, midnight feasts, dressing-up parties, sneaking out at night.

I asked where she had found it, and she said it had been in the cherrywood box. She admitted that she had forced the lock in the expectation of finding the missing brooch. Had she found it? I asked. She conceded that she had not but said the book unmasked the girl as a liar, and that is tantamount to being a thief.

I asked if there had been anything else in the box, and she said there was nothing except a photograph in a glazed frame showing the girl with her family.

I was dismayed at that turn of events for I knew how seriously the girl would take the invasion of her privacy.

I should have made her put the book back, but there seemed no point since the lock had been broken and there was no way to conceal that. However, I told her that what she had done was very wrong and she should apologise to the girl.

She snorted at that and said it was the girl who owed us an apology for the fantasy she had tried to impose on us.

When my younger daughter got back, her sister showed her the book, and they went through it finding stories and even actual phrases that the girl had used in describing her alleged adventures with her friends.

I told them that they were right to deplore the girl's lies but begged them to remember that although they did not have the material advantages that she had had, they had been brought up to be honest and truthful. Our 'guest' had been raised with different values.

When the girl got back with my wife, we listened to her going into the bedroom. After a few minutes there was a howl of anger and despair. She came rushing into the living-room and delivered a tirade of accusations and abuse at both my daughters. They said nothing, but when she paused for breath my elder daughter merely held up the book and said: *We know where all your lies came from.*

The girl's face went white. She said: *I hate you. I hate all of you. You're horrid and stupid and common.* Then she ran out of the room.

* * *

That week the director called me into his office and asked if I had ever had any reason to suspect that assets in cash, bonds, gold, etc, that had been located were not being fully reported. I tried to hide my unease and stuck to the line I had decided to adopt. No, I had never had any reason to suppose that. He looked as if he didn't believe me. I wondered why he had suddenly become suspicious and why he had chosen me as the person to interrogate. Was he putting the same question to others? Had my 'client', the wealthy lawyer, lodged an accusation against me with him?

The next day it was announced that there would be a new procedure. Whenever a 'client' revealed the existence of a safe or bank-deposit box or any portable assets, that fact would be reported to the director. He would deal with the matter and do so with a number of witnesses present 'in order to avoid even the appearance of wrong-doing'.

The head and his deputy did not conceal from myself and my colleagues that they were furious at this development, which they called 'a grave slur on our integrity'. They implied that they believed the director was himself looting the assets, though I'm sure they knew that was not the case.

* * *

The next day my younger daughter got home from school while everyone else was out and found the glass-framed photograph from the box sitting on the mantelpiece in the shared bedroom. When I arrived home she called me into the room to show me and said: *It takes up far too much room and it's so big that someone's going to knock it off and break it and if it's me, I know I'll get blamed for it.*

The photograph showed the girl sitting at the front of a group. Behind her were a middle-aged couple I assumed were her parents and a young man who must have been her brother. Everyone was looking at the camera except the girl, who was gazing at a small boy beside her who was, presumably, her other brother.

When the girl got home my daughter told her the photograph was intruding on shared space. The girl said: *It was your sister who stole it from my box. I'll put it there if I choose.*

There was a furious row, and I hurried into the room just in time to see the girl seize the photograph and smash it against the stone hearth of the fireplace. She tore the photograph from its shattered frame and ripped it across several times.

I told her I was shocked at her lack of respect for her family, and she glared at me in the most disconcerting manner. She was made to clean up the broken glass.

Later that day my wife showed me what she had found in the wastepaper-basket: the girl had thrown away the photograph of her family which she had torn up. I felt I had to confront her about it. I led her into the study and said: *I think you were very wrong to tear up that photograph and throw it away. It's not your parents' fault that they are not here to look after you.*

She hung her head and said sullenly: *I didn't.*

I said: *There's no point lying. I saw you tear it up.*

She said: *I kept the part I wanted.*

I didn't know what to make of that. My wife was sure she had seen the remnants of the whole family group: herself, her parents, and her brother.

A couple of days later my younger daughter was looking for something on the mantelpiece of the living-room when she found the brooch. My elder daughter insisted that she had not put it there and so would not apologise to the girl for her suspicions. The girl must have put it there herself, my daughter insisted, having realised that her theft had been found out. However, I remembered that my daughter did sometimes leave pieces of jewellery there, and I was pretty sure that she had done so and then forgotten it.

* * *

A few weeks after our conversation about the 'client' with the certified deposit, my so-called friend was promoted by the director to be deputy head of one of the other sections and moved into another office.

Though I was sorry he had been elevated above me, I was not unhappy to see him go. I was pretty sure it was his reward for incriminating our head. He himself was now safe from that man's vengeance, but I was not. Moreover, I was also in trouble with the director, who probably knew that I had failed to report the malfeasance. I couldn't stop myself speculating about my 'friend's' motives in advising me to try to blackmail the head. I now suspected he had urged me to do that in the knowledge that it would have ended in the unmasking of both the head and myself.

* * *

I managed to get to the girl's house on just a single Tuesday during this period, and once I was inside, the servant made no objection to my looking round. (I believe she realised that I would have made trouble for her if she had refused to let me inspect the house.) I went upstairs and verified that the safe was still intact. I came down and, before the servant realised I was there, had time to look at the opened bills that the girl had left. Apart from items like rates, electricity, and insurance I saw that some of the leading commercial figures in the father's community had made him very considerable loans that they were now calling in. The collateral he had given them appeared to be shares in the store. Before I could work out the details, the servant came back and I had to break off.

There were no letters or telegrams and, as always, the servant told me that she had heard nothing from the rest of the girl's family.

Discussing that fact later that day, my wife and I deplored the off-handedness of the girl's parents in not bothering to ensure the welfare of their daughter. In spite of the difficulties, they should have found a way to establish contact. We could not imagine being so negligent towards one of our children. Their lack of concern had presented us with a dilemma: what to do about the registration of the girl now that, as she kept reminding us, her fourteenth birthday was imminent. We decided to do nothing since our interpretation of the regulation suggested she did not need to register given that she had been under fourteen on the date when the requirement was announced. She fell into the category of young persons the date of whose compulsory registration would be given out in due course.

The reason why the girl kept talking of her imminent birthday had nothing to do with that regulation. She was dropping hints about the kind of birthday she wanted, and as far as we were able to, we made preparations for it. By now the prices of many foodstuffs were ridiculously high but I had saved some of my own coupons and had put aside some cash, and my wife sought out some bargains. We knew how important birthdays were to children of that age, and we were determined to do the best for her that circumstances permitted. I scrimped and saved, and by cutting out lunch two days a week, I managed to set aside enough coupons to buy the ingredients of a small cake.

I could not help reflecting that although the girl and I had brought plenty of valuable artefacts home, there were still many remaining in the house. Moreover, there was the safe, and if only I could gain access to it, I could use the cash, gold, and bonds that it presumably contained to pay myself back for the girl's upkeep and set aside some money to find alternative shelter for her. I thought how grateful the girl's father would be if I managed to rescue his portable assets.

* * *

The girl's birthday came and we celebrated the day as best we could given our reduced circumstances and the shortages imposed by rationing. I think we all managed to conceal our negative feelings about her. My wife made the cake, and we all gave her little presents.

It was obvious, however, that she was disappointed by our efforts. At the end of the day she thanked my wife and myself in a very small voice and without meeting our gaze.

* * *

Ironically, the girl had a sort of belated birthday present from the authorities, for on the very next day it was announced on the wireless that the Enemy had 'magnanimously' decreed that the Western Zone was being annexed as part of its own territory. That decision entailed that everyone in the Western Zone at the time of its creation would henceforth enjoy full rights of citizenship provided they met the qualifying criteria. I told the girl it meant her parents and younger brother were safe. I remember that her eyes filled with tears and she came over and gave me a fierce hug.

The Eastern Zone was now all that remained of our poor nation—though as if in mockery it continued to bear the ancient name of the whole country—and it was announced on that day that our city had been designated the new capital since the old one was now inside the territory of the Enemy.

We were cut off from our relatives there and, naturally, our annual visit was out of the question.

* * *

The following Wednesday, we were listening to the nine o'clock news when it was announced that all prisoners-of-war who were citizens of our country would be released and allowed to go home. The girl jumped up clapping her hands and skipped round the room in delight. Her brother would soon be back! She wanted to go to the house in a few days and said she expected to find him waiting for her. Then she shook her head and said wryly: *What a shame he just missed my birthday.*

We were all delighted as well. It meant she would soon be leaving us.

* * *

A couple of days later I was walking towards my office after lunch when the director's office-manager—a man to whom I had hardly ever spoken—came alongside me and started chatting about a certain violin-teacher whom I knew. He was a member of the girl's community and, until a few years ago, had taught my elder daughter for a couple of years. As we talked, the office-manager steered me into his office, which was just outside that of the director. The director himself came in and the manager said to him: *We were just*

talking about someone I believe you know, sir. I learned that the violin-teacher had, until the recent decree banning him from working
outside his own community, been giving the director's son lessons.
The director talked of how he was worried about him. He was, of
course, no longer able to earn his living by teaching, and with four
children and a wife to support, his plight was fairly desperate.

And yet, the manager put in thoughtfully, *he should be all right
because his brother-in-law owns a furniture factory in the Old City.* He
mentioned the man's name, and I remarked that he happened to be
a 'client' of mine.

The conversation ended and I went back to work. I would have
forgotten about it if it had not had such important consequences.

* * *

Now that I had begun to wonder if the girl's father really was as
wealthy as he appeared, I was desperately anxious to know if his
name was on the list being worked on by my head or his deputy. If it
was not, then it was likely that he had slipped through the net, and
that would be a huge relief because it meant he would not be investigated and the girl's whereabouts would not become an issue for the
authorities. He might be merely the nominal owner of the store or
have only a small share in it. And the fact he was being dunned for
large sums of money certainly did not of itself mean he was bankrupt.

My colleagues and I had almost finished working through the
list of the 'protected community's' richest one hundred and fifty
businessmen and would soon embark on the next batch of returns
which had been piling up. The threshold had been lowered to the
point where there were more than two thousand for us to process,
but we would not need to be as thorough in these new cases, of
course, since the assets would be fewer and less complex.

In the hope that I might be able to seize the chance to look at
the lists being worked on by my head or his deputy, I was keeping a
careful watch on their movements in order to spot an opportunity
to go into their offices.

* * *

A few days after that, the director's office-manager accosted me in the street as I was leaving the building at the end of the day. He said he wanted to have a little chat with me in private and led me to a bar in a back-street that I had never visited. When we were sitting with a drink in front of us, he told me that there was a complication relating to one of my 'clients'. It was the owner of the furniture-factory whom we had mentioned the other day because he was the brother-in-law of the violin-teacher whom the director and I both knew. I told him I had just sent his completed accounts to the director to be signed off.

He nodded and to my surprise produced my set of accounts from his briefcase. It consisted of four pages and the last one had been signed by the director.

The manager pointed out the second page which listed transactions relating to one of the 'client's' bank accounts and indicated one item. It was the recent transfer of quite a large sum into another account. I had recorded the name and account-number of the recipient, and it would have been the responsibility of one of my colleagues to track it in relation to that individual's accounts.

That, he told me, *is an account controlled by the violin-teacher, although the name is not his. His brother-in-law was helping him financially but as you see, the transfer was made several months after the cut-off date before which such transactions need not be traced. The director would like you to remove that page and re-type it, changing the date of that transfer to a date prior to the cut-off point. He wants this act of generosity towards a struggling family-man to stand. Otherwise, as you know, the money will be confiscated.*

This was an astonishing suggestion. If it were ever detected, I would be in serious trouble. I pointed out that the carbon copy kept by my head of section in his files would show the truth, and he assured me that nobody would ever have any reason to look at it.

He said: *The director will be anxious to show his gratitude towards you.*

I took that as a hint that I, too, might be promoted to be the head of a section. In that case I would have nothing to fear from my present head.

I agreed to do it. Two days later I handed the manager the revised set of accounts.

* * *

No sooner had we dealt with one birthday than the next was upon us, for my younger daughter's fourteenth birthday was now only a few weeks away and despite the circumstances, my wife and I were determined to make it a fittingly memorable occasion.

It was now that it became impossible to blind myself to the fact that my younger daughter was behaving uncharacteristically. She indulged in tantrums and started answering back in a manner she had never shown before. The wartime conditions obviously played a role in that, but it was also a reaction to the presence of the girl and the way she was holding the family in thrall. My wife now resented her so much that she could hardly bring herself to put food in front of her.

I was therefore not completely surprised when my wife told me a few days later that she wanted to take our younger daughter to a remote village a day's journey away where old family friends of hers lived. She and our child would stay there until the girl had left the apartment. I pointed out that we could not afford it and that there were now severe restrictions on travel and change of residence. What would they do there? How could I send them money? How would our daughter be educated? I could not bear the thought of their going away on such terms. If I had sent them away to safety because of the political situation, I could have endured it, but if they left now, it would be because they believed—or my wife at least believed—that I had put them in danger and somewhere else would be safer.

Eventually she realised I was right and abandoned the project.

* * *

After a few days, our prisoners-of-war started arriving in the city—gaunt young men still in their uniforms which were often torn and blood-stained. The son of the tailor's family on our second floor was one of them, and there was an impromptu party on the stairs to welcome him home—which none of our household attended because I had decided we should keep to ourselves as far as possible.

The girl kept pestering me to let her go to the house and see if her brother was there or had left a message with neighbours. I wasn't prepared to take her, but I did continue to pass the house every few days and noticed no sign that anything had changed.

* * *

All this time the girl's behaviour was becoming more and more unacceptable. She was refusing to take part in the preparations for my daughter's birthday and would even leave the room if that subject was being discussed. It was clear to all of us that her envy of my daughter and resentment that her birthday was being taken so much more seriously than hers, were too strong to control.

It was on the day of my daughter's birthday that something happened at work which was potentially very serious for me.

That afternoon I waited until everyone had left our complex of offices. Then I went into the room next door which was used by the deputy. I located the file that I wanted which I hoped would tell me how rich the girl's father was and ideally where he and his wife were. To my dismay I found inside the file a sealed envelope labelled 'list No. 5 of individuals with assets above the limit'. I would have to open it and that would be difficult to conceal. I found a letter-opener and began to cut it in such way that I would be able to seal it again without it being too obvious.

I had examined nearly the whole document without finding the name I was looking for and was holding the paper in my hands when the deputy walked into the room. He had forgotten his cigarette-lighter and come back for it. I had been so intent on my task that I had not heard him.

He demanded to know why I was in his office and what I wanted with that document. Why had I committed what he called the 'outrageous' act of opening a sealed envelope?

I blustered and told him I wanted to cross check one of my 'clients' with one of his who was my man's nephew. Foolishly, I hadn't properly prepared such an excuse and I stumbled and failed to produce appropriate names and I could see that he didn't believe me.

He reached for the telephone and summoned the head. We didn't speak until he came into the room.

He heard my stumbling explanation and just said: *There'll be consequences.* He jerked his head to indicate that I should leave.

I guessed that they were making the assumption that I was trying to find a way to steal money. I wondered if I could think of something that would mislead them into believing that but without putting myself in jeopardy. I failed.

Worryingly, the girl's father appeared on none of the four lists I had seen. Of course, I had not seen Lists 4 and 6 or the whole of List 5.

* * *

I had an anxious evening but had to conceal my emotions because of the birthday celebrations. I had decided to tell my wife nothing since there was no point in worrying her when it might turn out not to be necessary. It was frustrating that I had not quite reached the end of the list when I had been interrupted. The name might be on it or on the list held by the head, but there was no possibility I would be able to find out now.

My elder daughter had made a new party-dress as a gift for her sister, and my wife had bought a fine piece of costume-jewellery that looked more expensive than it was and went well with the new dress. The sour note was the sulky, ungracious attitude of the girl, who made it clear she resented everything being done for the benefit of the birthday girl. She had given her nothing, which was forgivable given the circumstances, but I could see my daughter was upset.

Unfortunately my wife commented on that and the girl said: *I didn't need to make her a gift. You all saved your coupons for her for months. She's being given everything. A thousand times more than you gave me.*

She ran out of the room. We all stared at each other in despair. I didn't think we could bear her tempers and tantrums much longer.

* * *

The next morning I was summoned by the head and found his deputy sitting beside him. I had had time to elaborate an explanation that I hoped might be convincing, and said I was afraid there might be some duplication so that the same name appeared on his list as well as mine, and I had merely been checking that. The head brushed that aside and made it plain he thought I was trying to skim some of the assets I was investigating—perhaps by taking a bribe to turn a blind eye to something I had discovered. I was pretty sure that was precisely what he and his deputy had been doing themselves.

He told me he was not going to institute dismissal proceedings but would send me a written warning about the matter which would be copied to our superiors, and if I ever stepped out of line again, I would at best find myself looking for another post.

Later I realised that what had saved me from dismissal was almost certainly the head's fear that if he had tried to sack me, I might have insisted on an investigation which, whether or not it cleared me, might have brought to light his and his deputy's nefarious activities.

I was still in grave danger. At a point in the future, when it would be too late to carry out a full investigation of the documentation, the head and his deputy would be able to use that letter to have me dismissed on the flimsiest pretext. I was now in their power and would not be able to refuse to do what they demanded.

* * *

The next day the deadline arrived for members of the girl's community over fourteen to register. I would have forgotten about it were it not that on the ten o'clock news that evening—the procedure for registration having closed at six o'clock—the authorities announced a number of new regulations.

The girls and my wife had gone to bed. I remember sitting alone and thinking about the implications of what I had just heard. It had been announced that the country was now in a 'transitional' stage and during this period 'guidance' would be offered to the national population. Every employer was obliged to check the identity-card of every employee and if it indicated membership of the 'protected community', to take appropriate action. That also applied to private individuals in relation to their domestic staff. All employees—including servants—were required to look at the identity-card of their employer and to leave immediately if it indicated membership of that community. Furthermore, notices were going to be put up indicating if a shop or other kind of business was owned by one of them. The most worrying clause was the final one: a manifest would be published of known members of the community who had failed to register.

* * *

The next day there was a bombshell. Our director was arrested! For several days that was all we knew. Then we heard he had been accused of accepting a bribe from one of the 'clients'. Eventually the details emerged and I was horrified: the 'client' concerned was the owner of the furniture-factory! It was my changing of the date that was at issue. It was assumed the director had changed the date in return for a bribe from the man and the proof that it was he who had done so, was that the carbon-copy showed the true date.

I saw the whole conspiracy in a flash: the director's office-manager had been lying when he said the owner of the furniture-factory was the violin-teacher's brother-in-law. There was no connection between the two men. The director himself had known nothing about what I had done and was entirely innocent.

The head of my section had concocted the plot with the director's office-manager in order to destroy his superior in revenge and in the hope of being promoted to his post and, he imagined, getting his hands on the wealth he assumed the director had been stealing.

I was not surprised to be summoned before the head and his deputy and told that when asked, I should say I had sent the accounts to the director in their original form and therefore it must have been he who, on his own initiative, had falsified them. I had to go along with that because the truth would not have been believed and my stating the facts would have destroyed me. I hardly needed the head to remind me, as he did, that I already had a black mark against my name and if another misdemeanour were found, the consequences would be dire.

I hated to do it, but I had no choice. So when I was required to make a formal statement to the investigating authorities, I said what I had been told to. There was no reason for anyone to doubt my word or to believe the director's protest that he had not touched the accounts.

* * *

Later that day I walked past the department store. It had a notice in every window telling the public it was owned by a member of the despised community and that as loyal patriots, customers might therefore prefer not to patronise it.

I was now alarmed. Since the authorities knew the identity of the family who at least at some point had owned the store and must be aware that the father was in the former Western Zone, they must also know about the house, and if they had visited it they would have learned that the girl was absent from it because she had moved in with another family. If they had not already gone to the house and talked to the servant, it could only be a matter of time before they did so.

I assumed the father's name was on the list of a hundred and fifty names. But there was another possibility: the authorities had a record telling them that the family were elsewhere. If that was so, would they know the girl was not with her parents? Would they bother about her if they did? And if the servant were questioned, would she be able to reveal enough information about me for the authorities to identify me and find the girl? Having found her, would they take some action against me?

Late into the night I talked over this new development with my wife, and we agreed it was getting more and more awkward to have the girl living with us—especially if at some future date we would have to account for her presence to the authorities. We had broken no regulations—or so we believed at the time—but we had perhaps offended against their spirit by failing to register her when she reached fourteen—though that was not compulsory. On that argument, the girl should go back to the house as soon as possible. And yet at any moment her family might return, and then it would be such a shame after all the expense and inconvenience we had incurred if they found we had simply dumped her back home with a surly and dishonest servant simply in order to avoid embarrassment.

All depended therefore on what if anything the servant could reveal about who the girl had gone to.

Then I had an idea and my wife approved of it. We had no telephone, of course, but I would ring the girl's house from my office and talk to the servant and pretend to be an official asking about the family and its present location. I would press her on the topic of the girl's whereabouts and find out how much she knew.

The next day I waited until lunchtime when nobody was in the office and dialled the number. There was no answer. I tried ringing many times during the next hour without success. The next day I tried again when I had the place to myself. No response. Was the servant no longer there? Or was she, for some reason, choosing not to answer the telephone? That seemed anomalous given that she must be expecting to hear from her employer. It also meant the girl's brother was not at the house.

* * *

Very cautiously I asked one or two colleagues about the director's fate. That must have got back to the head of section because the following day he summoned me to his office and said: *I hear you've been asking about your friend the former director. If you want him, you'll find him in the cattle-market.*

Assuming he had been reduced to some lowly position like inspector of slaughterhouses, I asked: *Has he been demoted?*

The head smiled. *No, you'll find him quite high up.*

That afternoon after work I walked to the Old City where the cattle-market was. I had not had any reason to enter it since the invasion. Once inside the old walls I walked around, and everything seemed normal. There were the usual shops and street-markets. I reached the eastern gate beyond which was the big square with the slaughterhouses on the further side and beyond them the cattle-market with its pens for unloading pigs and cattle from the trains which ran alongside it.

I went up to one of the slaughtermen in his blood-stained leather apron and asked for the director by name. He looked astonished and shrugged and hurried away. I accosted another. He pursed his lips and pointed towards a row of telegraph poles nearby. I now realised that there were two bodies hanging from them. Both had a big yellow badge attached to their jackets.

I went closer and saw that one of them had a placard round his neck. The text was: *I robbed my own people with this enemy of our nation.*

I forced myself to look at the face. With the mouth wrenched open and the upper lip exposing the teeth in what looked like an angry snarl, it was hideously like the head of a slaughtered pig hanging in a butcher's shop. I didn't recognise it at first and it took some time for me to make out the resemblance to the man I had known. I turned and walked away as stiffly as a wooden puppet. If that could happen to an innocent man, nobody was safe. And I didn't try to hide from myself that I had helped to bring it about. I was part of this horror.

I assumed the other corpse was that of the factory-owner.

I hadn't known that the director had even been on trial—let alone condemned to death.

* * *

When I got home I told my wife we should delay no longer and I would take the girl home the next day—a Saturday—however much she protested. So after supper we got her alone and talked to her about how much more comfortable she would be at her own house than in our poky little apartment which had no garden. She would have a servant to attend to all her whims and a large house to invite her friends to. (Assuming she had any, which I now doubted.) My daughters and I, I said, would visit her often. (I doubted that, too.) And when her parents and brother arrived home, how glad they would be to find her there. Her brother might be there already, I reminded her. (I said that even though I did not believe it since he had not answered the phone.)

The girl was deeply upset at being—as she put it—thrown out, and she talked of the servant's hatred of her. We saw that as an attempt to resist our decision, and we were not shaken by her tears.

* * *

So after breakfast the next day I set off with the girl. She had packed her suitcase and I was carrying it. We got out at the nearest tram-stop and then on an impulse, I hired a taxi. It was partly because of the weight of the suitcase, but I had a vague idea it might be wise to conceal the girl until I was sure how things were at the house.

I left her sitting in the taxi a few doors away from her home and walked up to it as if I were intending to pass it. The door had boards nailed across it and plastered over them was a poster. I stopped to read it: *Warning: This property is now under the guardianship of the Department of Protection and unauthorised entry will incur prosecution.*

A friendly maid-servant polishing the brass knocker of the house next door noticed my interest and started telling me the story.

Three days earlier, a taxi arrived very early in the morning. Knowing that the family were not in residence, a servant in the house opposite had looked out of the window. She had seen the servant of the girl's family emerge from the house with a trunk and two suitcases. She had been too greedy, and as the driver was loading one of the suitcases into the boot it fell open and its contents were scattered on the pavement. The watching woman saw ornaments and pieces of china that were obviously of great value before the servant managed to stuff them back in the suitcase. She then had an argument with the driver, whose suspicions had clearly been aroused. At that point the watching woman ran into the breakfast-room and told her employer, a doctor, what she had seen. By now the taxi and its occupant had driven away, but the doctor rang the police. They had rushed to the station but were too late to catch the servant, who must have got away on a train departing almost immediately. Unfortunately, several trains had left within a few minutes of each other, and it was impossible to establish which she had taken. The woman was thought to have gone back to her village of origin in some remote rural district. Since nobody knew the name of the village, nothing more could be done. The worst of it was that the authorities had now been alerted to the fact that a handsome house owned by a wealthy member of the minority community was standing empty and they had sealed it.

At that moment I heard a sound and glanced round. To my annoyance the girl was getting out of the taxi. I turned so the maid could not see what I was doing and made a gesture with my hand to tell her to get back into it. The maid had glanced at the taxi when I did, but I wasn't sure if she had seen the girl or recognised her if she had.

The maid said the servant at the girl's house had been grumbling for months about having received no wages and had been saying she was legally and morally entitled to sell items from the house in order to feed herself so she could stay there and protect the property.

I thanked her and walked on. In order to conceal the fact it had been that house I was interested in, I circled the block and got back to the taxi and boarded it. I ordered it to drive back to the tram-stop. The girl began to shower me with questions, but I indicated she should not speak until we were alone.

Once we were standing at the stop, I told her what I had learned. She was torn between delight that the hated servant had vanished and anguish that the house had been looted by her. She was very upset at hearing that there was no sign of her brother having returned.

She was, however, relieved when I told her about the poster and she learned that the property was now under the protection of the authorities. She longed to know what had been stolen and whether the safe had been compromised and her mother's jewels purloined.

The maid had not mentioned the brother. I was beginning to fear he had not been returned with the rest of the prisoners-of-war— perhaps because he was either wounded or had died.

When we reached the door of our apartment I rang the bell. My wife opened it, but as soon as she saw the girl she screamed and slammed the door in our faces. The girl seemed to catch her hysteria and began to cry. I knocked and there was no response and so I increased the volume of the knocking as far as I dared because I did not want to alert the neighbours below. At last I persuaded my wife to open the door and she did so with the chain attached. We talked through the crack in the door.

My wife kept saying: *Why have you brought her back?* I told her I'd explain once we were inside.

I heard a door opening below us and no sound of footsteps. Someone in one of the other apartments was standing on the landing and listening.

Still refusing to let us enter, my wife faltered out that she had just heard on the wireless something that had been announced that day. This was why she was so horrified to see the girl. She had believed we had got rid of the problem and here I was bringing her back.

She explained that the clarification of the regulation she had just heard stipulated that children from the 'protected community' had to register when they reached fourteen whenever that happened and not just if it occurred before the earlier date given out. In other words, I realised in horror, we had misinterpreted the regulation, and the girl should have been registered several months ago.

We were speaking in whispers, but my wife's were hoarse and too loud for safety. I pointed out in a whisper that the more of a scene we created the more notice the neighbours would take of us.

My wife unhooked the chain and let us in. The girl, weeping and distraught, ran into the room she shared with my younger daughter.

When my wife and I were alone I urged her to stop worrying. I said the authorities were issuing so many new laws and regulations that the agencies which were supposed to enforce them could not possibly keep up and my own department was an example of that. I pointed out that the regulation promulgated several months ago had said children had to be registered by their parents. We were not the girl's parents or even her guardians and therefore were not guilty of failing to register her.

That reassured her a little. Then I told her there was good news from my visit to the house. From what the friendly maid next door had said, it was clear that the servant stole the valuables before the authorities came and so there was no reason to suppose she had given them any information about the girl or her connection with ourselves. Moreover, given that she must have anticipated after her accident with the suitcase and her argument with the driver, that the theft would become known to the police, it was extremely unlikely she would ever reappear since she would almost certainly be charged with that crime. She had stolen from the state, rather than the girl's family, and the state would prosecute her. That meant there was no means by which the link between the house and ourselves could be established.

That was all true, but the fear I had—and which I did not share with my wife—was that one of the neighbours might have mentioned to the authorities that the girl had not been in the former capital with her parents when hostilities began, but in the city, and that she had not been living at her own house for the last few months.

This raised the possibility they might put her on the manifest of persons they wished to find. And then it must be only a matter of time before someone connected with the school told them of her friendship with my younger daughter.

It was horribly clear to me that since the girl had stayed with us past the age of fourteen without registering, I had breached the regulations; and I knew that if my superiors found out I had fallen foul of even the most trivial ordinance, they would seize the opportunity to take dismissal proceedings against me. This would not be regarded as a trivial breach but a major infraction.

There was nothing to be gained by sharing that with my wife. What I had said about our not being her parents or guardians was, I feared, irrelevant.

I was now worried about another possibility. Had the friendly maid seen and even recognised the girl when she briefly got out of the taxi? If so, and if she mentioned that to the authorities, had I said or revealed anything to her that might enable them to find me? I didn't think so, but it was possible that someone passing by, whom I had not even noticed, had known who I was. Or that I had been recognised during my frequent visits to the house. After all, in my work I dealt with many individuals.

And there was something else on my mind. I could not stop thinking about the contents of the safe. I assumed the servant had not managed to open it—and it was so big and heavy that she had certainly not prised it intact out of the wall and taken it with her even inside a trunk! If the picture on the wall was still concealing it, then the authorities had presumably not found it. So inside it lay jewels and cash and gold and financial instruments that were worth a huge amount of money and which could, unlike the valuables the girl had brought, be used immediately or easily converted into cash.

That night I lay awake for hours thinking about the danger I had brought upon my family. What I had seen in the cattle-market was a warning of how severe the consequences of my actions could be. I had contributed to the death of the director by a very minor breach of the rules, but what I had done by hiding the girl was much more serious.

* * *

I decided to question the girl—very subtly and indirectly—about the safe. So that evening I invited her into my study and raised the topic. I told her its contents would make life very much easier for her if she could gain possession of them. I asked her if anybody apart from her father knew the combination number, and she said that as far as she was aware, nobody did. That seemed to settle the matter—especially since I assumed it was impossible to get into the house anyway. I made that point, and she astonished me by saying she had a set of keys. I recalled she had rung the bell when we went back, so that was surprising. She said she had done it so the servant would not realise she had them. I reflected that keys were of no use since the front-door was boarded up.

Thinking about what she had said a little later, however, I was struck by her having referred to 'a set' rather than just 'a key'. I tackled her again and she said the key to the back-door was also on the key-ring she had. That put the matter in a new light. If the back-door had not been boarded up, I might be able to enter the house by that route.

I remembered the safe's combination-lock involved eight numbers. I asked her to write down the dates of birth of all five members of her family. I had the idea of trying out those figures since the year, month, and day would be precisely eight digits and it was likely her father had used one of them.

* * *

The next morning I had proof—nearly certain proof, at least—that our concierge had heard my wife's altercation with me or at least had been told about it. I was leaving the building with my wife and the girl, who were going into the commercial centre to do some shopping, when the woman tapped on the glass of her hatch to stop me.

The concierge was a particularly inquisitive representative of her species. Her apartment had an internal window or hatch onto the lobby overlooking the entrance so she could see all arrivals and departures. There was a sliding grille which was pushed open when she was 'on duty' which was from roughly eight in the morning to any time up to midnight that she chose, though she usually closed the hatch at nine or ten. She was brusque with the other occupants but always polite to me to the point of being excessively deferential, and that made me suspect she was filled with resentment towards me on account of my higher standing.

She now slid the grille open and said she needed to see the girl's identity-card. I asked on what grounds, and she said the police had announced concierges were now required to check the identity-card of all strangers and report any irregularities. I said that I had not heard anything about such an order and that there were no irregularities to report. She smiled in the particularly unpleasant way she had and looked at the girl and said there was something that puzzled her. The joiner's wife had said that I told her she was my wife's niece. Then she said: *And what's so strange is that your wife mentioned to the tailor's wife that she was* your *niece.*

I laughed in what I hoped was a convincingly light-hearted manner and said that the joiner's wife must have misheard me. The child was a cousin of mine and because she was a generation younger, we referred to her as our niece. She blinked and seemed to be thinking about that. Then she repeated her demand to see the identity-card, and I continued to refuse. She shook her head sadly and said she might have to report me to the police. I called her bluff and told her I would be delighted if she did so. I had gambled on her being afraid to bother them on a matter that might turn out to be of no significance.

As soon as we were out of the building I reminded the girl that if she was ever asked for her identity, she must always give the first and second name of my cousin and her address. And I impressed upon her that she must never show her identity-card to the concierge or to anyone else.

I said that the concierge was an inquisitive and spiteful woman who wanted to make a nuisance of herself, and we should not allow her to take any further liberties. I was worried, however. I suspected she was not lying about her right to see identity-cards but was exaggerating and anticipating in the sense that someone in the police had told her such a regulation was about to be introduced.

I did not say to my wife that the identity-card would reveal, if the concierge were clever enough to spot it, that the girl's surname showed she belonged to the community and was over fourteen and therefore should have one of the new ones. If she ever had to show the card, we might all be in some difficulty. I had reasons for supposing that the concierge had access to information about the police. I knew her son drank in a sordid neighbourhood bar which was frequented by members of the auxiliary police, and he might well have picked up from them gossip about the future intentions of the authorities. The auxiliary police were untrained men who worked alongside the ordinary police, whose loyalty to their new masters was not entirely trusted, and who were recruited on the basis of their 'patriotism', which meant their willingness to help the Enemy to control the population by intimidation and spying.

* * *

The next day at work I kept thinking about the problem that the girl represented. As I saw it, our act of generosity combined with a misunderstanding of one of the hailstorm of new regulations, had put us in an awkward situation. Yet it wasn't our responsibility. We were not her parents or even relatives of hers.

I discussed it with my wife that evening. I said we could not rely on the girl's parents returning any time in the near future. Nor could we count on a new school being opened which could take responsibility for the girl. I said we must find some other relatives of the girl. She was their problem and not ours. They would have to take her into their home and then deal with the fact that she had failed to register by the deadline.

My wife agreed but said she feared the girl had no relatives. So we tackled her straightaway on the subject of her family. She seemed strangely resistant to saying anything about anyone other than her parents and her brothers and was adamant that there were no uncles or aunts or grandparents to whom she could go.

Did she have any links with local people in her own community?

Now she abandoned the pretence that she and her family existed in a giddy social whirl and insisted that she knew nobody to whom she could turn for food and shelter. Her family had not lived in the city long, and since her parents did not practise their religion, they had not met people at places of worship.

In response to our questions the girl started whining about how she wanted to go and find her parents and younger brother. I was tempted to give her some cash and a small suitcase of clothes and let her go, but she would have been stopped before she had got very far and the trail would have led back to us.

However, she made a good point when she wondered what would happen if her parents—or even her brother when he was released from the prisoner-of-war camp—came to the house and found her gone? How would they locate her? She wanted to leave a letter for them at the house giving them our address.

I bit back my main objection to that and merely pointed out that it might take some time for her father to gain permission to re-enter the house since it had passed into the custody of the state. She said in that case she would write to him at the store. No purpose would be served by alarming the girl, so I just made the same point: during her father's absence the store was being administered by someone else and the letter would probably go astray.

My younger daughter had come in a few minutes earlier and heard the last part of our conversation about how the girl's brother or parents could locate her. Now she asked if there was any place that her family used to go to together—a restaurant or a café?

The girl's eyes sparkled and she said that often on a Friday her father met her and her brothers and mother when they all left school and work, and they had a celebration to mark the end of the working week. They patronised a certain Viennese-style café facing the cathedral, arriving there at five o'clock. They would drink hot chocolate and eat cakes, and then their driver would pick them up and they would go home for dinner. It was the one time that they all ate together—if her parents had no social engagement for that evening.

That's perfect, my clever daughter said. *In that case, all we have to do is put some sort of token on the front of the house to point towards the café.*

I grasped it now, but it had to be spelled out to the girl. If we pasted a notice advertising the café on the boarded up door, it would indicate to any of her family who saw it that they should meet her at that rendezvous at the usual time.

She agreed but was worried her brother might not recognise the significance of the notice since he had long ago stopped coming to the café with the rest of them and might not remember its name in connection with the family's custom.

The next morning on the way into the office I took a route that let me pass the Viennese café, which was a big and well-known establishment. (Of course, it—indeed the whole street—is no longer there.) I went in and sat down and drank a coffee and took a handful of business cards as I left. After work I went to the house and, with the nail and tacks I had brought, pinned a couple of the cards to the wooden boards across the front-door. It would look as if someone had opportunistically advertised their business in the way that was done all over the city.

* * *

Thinking about the whole issue that night, it seemed to me that the girl had slipped through the system and the solution was to put her back into it. But I could not see how to do that without the authorities finding out about her non-registration and blaming me for it. It was possible that would be connected with my having looked at the file, and if that happened, I could not predict how gravely the matter would be viewed.

Yet perhaps non-registration was not such a serious issue. It might be regarded as a technicality. And it might be one that could very easily be resolved. New identity-cards were being issued in large numbers every day for children in the girl's community reaching fourteen. If one could be issued for the girl in exchange for her old one, nobody would ever know that it had been done some time later than it should have been. The only obstacle was that the person doing the issuing would see that the date of birth fell outside the legal requirement. But surely that person could easily pretend not to have noticed? It came to me in a flash. It was as easy as that! One of the officials might be persuaded by one means or another to make the exchange, and the girl would immediately be safely inside the system.

I told my wife my idea. She was doubtful it could be done and moreover raised a difficulty I had overlooked. Which address should we choose for her on the new identity-card? Giving hers and letting her stay on in our apartment would mean that we were breaking the law. But putting our address would make the girl inescapably our responsibility if her parents for some reason failed to claim her. After lengthy debate we opted for her family house. We would at a later point have to face the question of reporting to the authorities that she was, in fact, lodging with us.

But how, my wife wondered, was I going to get an official to make the exchange?

I had remembered that the man I ran into a few months back while I was buying cigars was now working in the Department of Protection. He was a former colleague in my own department, and we had been on friendly terms—though not friendly enough to have kept in touch when he was transferred to a different department in another building.

I decided I would very cautiously sound him out about the possibility of helping me with my problem. After all, he only needed to obtain a blank identity-card and issue it in the girl's name—which was happening all the time—and then ensure that the record entered the system.

The next morning I tried to telephone him. I could only do so when the office was deserted at lunchtime and, of course, his extension was not answered because at that time he was himself at lunch. This went on for several days until at last I managed to speak to him.

When we had got the greetings out of the way and the apologies for not having kept in touch and the enquiries about each other's health and that of each member of both our families, he asked me if there was anything he could do for me.

In a very roundabout manner I raised the problem, saying that a friend of mine knew a family belonging to the minority community who were therefore required to apply for new identity-cards but whose daughter had somehow failed to register by the deadline. I wondered if anything could be done to sort the matter out with the minimum of repercussions. My former colleague replied after a lengthy pause, saying he hadn't understood what I meant. I realised he feared that he was being entrapped—that someone was listening on another line while I attempted to compromise him. That horrified me. I had not realised the issue was of such significance nor that such fears could be entertained.

I suggested we should meet 'just to catch up after so long' and he agreed, and we arranged an appointment for the following evening in a bar we both knew.

* * *

When I spotted my former colleague I could see how nervous he was. He kept looking round as if he feared someone was listening to us. He understood precisely what I was asking him, and he said it could be done but it would cost him a great deal of extra work in his own time. I had not grasped, he said, that it was much less simple than merely inserting the girl into the system. If he just created a new identity-card and recorded the details, it was virtually certain that the discrepancy in the date of birth would be noticed by someone further along the line who entered details into the records. What he would have to do was to get access to the actual records and insert hers in the right position. Since he had no reason to deal with those documents, he would be taking a huge risk. In short, I realised that I was being told I would have pay him a considerable sum. My belief that this was a simple matter which could be done as a favour was absurd.

He asked who the girl was, and fortunately I had anticipated that question. I had been worried that if I avoided answering he would not agree to help me. On the other hand, if I revealed her identity, I gave him too much power over me before he had made any matching commitment. I therefore gave him an answer that only partly identified her. I said: *My friend said that her father is a prominent businessman in the city.*

My former colleague asked: *Why did her father not register her?*

I said: *As it happened, the girl was not in the city at the relevant time and her father assumed she had registered where she was.*

Unfortunately, he then offered me seven or eight names of prominent businessmen belonging to the community and asked if the man was one of them?

He was, and I admitted that but refused to say which of the names was his.

That, he said gravely, *seriously complicates the matter.*

I should have realised that the girl's father, as one of the community's apparently wealthiest businessmen, was obviously of interest to the authorities. It had been naïve of me to fail to see that. Therefore his daughter's record would, indeed, be subject to close scrutiny. He would be running a huge risk.

We talked some more and eventually a figure emerged. It was the equivalent of six weeks of my salary! There was absolutely no possibility I could afford to pay that. I tried to negotiate, but he insisted that the risk was too great to be worth taking for a lower figure.

I told him I would pass on his offer to my friend but that I doubted if he could manage the sum, and after a few rather forced exchanges we parted.

I had failed, and worse than that, I began to wonder if the man would suspect I had tried to lure him into committing an indiscretion in order to gain credit by denouncing him. I tried to imagine what I would do if I were in his position. If I really believed that someone had tried to entrap me, I would have only one recourse: to expose him to the authorities before he denounced me. All that would restrain me would be the fear he might be able to demonstrate I had been prepared to entertain the offer to commit an offence. Would my former colleague be afraid that his agreeing to meet me in the bar would of itself suggest he had gone along with my invitation to impropriety? Or would he be deterred by the suspicion that I had planted a colleague to watch us? And that led me to wonder if *he* had arranged to have someone observe *us*.

That night and all the next day I went over and over the issue again and again. By the third day I was beginning to feel safe because my former colleague would have known that he had to act quickly if he was going to get in first.

As one worry receded—without vanishing entirely—another began to take its place. Why had the bribe been so high? This was a piece of documentation relating to a child that we had been talking about—a mere technical matter of a missed date. Was more at issue than I realised? Now it struck me that my former colleague had reeled off those seven or eight names very quickly and without having to think. What were the implications of that? Was he personally taking an interest in the wealthiest members of the community?

Was there something he knew by virtue of his position inside the Department of Protection that I did not? Something that perhaps he assumed I did know, which was why he had proposed such an exorbitant figure?

I told my wife what had occurred, and we agreed that the sum asked was too high to pay. Unfortunately, because I had raised the issue of money, she said she had been thinking about the valuables the girl had brought from her house, and she believed we should sell them. I objected that it would be theft.

To my regret, my wife told our elder daughter about that conversation, and she supported her immediately and passionately.

I had to agree. So the next day I took some of the more portable items to the nearest street-market. I found that there were no buyers. There was, I was told again and again, no market for luxuries like that since so many people had already sold what precious items they possessed. A diamond ring could be bought for the price of a few kilos of cabbages.

* * *

Since it was possible that a member of the girl's family had spotted the coded message I had fixed to the front door, we needed to start going to the Viennese café on Friday evenings.

So that Friday I took my wife and both my daughters and the girl to the café at five o'clock. We had to appear to be an ordinary family party—though I feared we looked too shabby to be typical of the customers there. The girl sat where she could see the door the whole time and watched eagerly every time it opened.

The proprietor was present, and he came over when the waiter had taken our order and greeted the girl by name. She began to introduce me, but I quickly interrupted her before she uttered my name and in order to disguise my intention, made a great performance of rising and shaking hands warmly with the man. When he asked my name I pretended not to hear him and talked rapidly to prevent the girl saying it. We chatted and he seemed perfectly friendly and asked the girl where the rest of her family were. She told him she was hoping they would arrive at any moment, but the last she had heard was that her brother was in a prisoner-of-war camp and her parents and other brother were staying with friends in what used to be the Western Zone. He shook his head in sympathy at that point, but the girl didn't seem to notice.

We stayed until after six, and the girl made a fuss about leaving even as late as that.

* * *

Money was becoming more and more of a worry since prices were rising rapidly while my reduced salary remained the same. Even the visits to the café—which now became a regular weekly event—involved paying very high prices for ices and coffees.

The first time we went there I made a note of the bill in my pocket-book, and a moment later I realised that the girl was looking over my shoulder. She was in some ways observant and acute though in academic matters and anything abstract or intellectual, she was slow-witted. That apparent paradox had struck me, and I had worked out that she was very sharp in anything which directly concerned her and especially the gratification of her desires, but she had no curiosity about matters that seemed otherwise irrelevant. In this, she contrasted strikingly with my bright, inquisitive, younger daughter. And that characteristic—the obsession with money and the self-interestedness—was, I considered, very typical of her community

As we walked back to the tram-stop, the girl came alongside me and asked why I had written down the amount of the bill. I told her that because of my accountancy background, it was my habit to keep a note of all household expenses. She looked as if this answer had not satisfied her.

Later that evening she came into my study and questioned me about it again. Eventually I told her I was noting down what she was costing us for her food and so on. She took it badly. She said

I was just trying to make money out of her. I was going to present her father with a grossly inflated bill. All we cared about was money.

This was so unfair and so ironic coming from her that I lost my temper. I told her she should be grateful that we had taken her in. I pointed out that she must have seen how many abandoned children there now were who had been reduced to begging in the streets. If we had not helped her she might well be in that situation. She answered that we had done it only to curry favour with her father, and she threw in my face the old canard about my hoping that he would reward me with a well-paid job. I said something quite harsh, and she ran into her room.

* * *

I stayed in the study for the next couple of hours. Because I was so worried about money I could not stop thinking about the safe in the girl's house. If I could get some of the cash it contained, I could pay the bribe to have my former colleague regularise the girl's relations with the authorities. It was in a sense the girl's money, and so taking it in order to help her was morally justifiable.

Of course, even if the safe were still concealed and intact, I did not know the combination and therefore would not be able to open it unless the girl's father had used one of the family's birthdates as the combination. I found the sheet on which the girl had written them and copied out each of them using all the different formats I could think of: day, month, year; year month, day; each of those in reverse order; etc. Assuming I could get into the house, it would take me a long time to go through all of them.

However, merely establishing that the safe was still there, and had not been discovered and either removed or opened by the authorities, would be the first step. At the same time, there was no point in raising the girl's hopes if nothing was going to come of it, so I was unwilling to ask her for the keys. I did not need to since I knew where she kept them.

On an impulse I decided to make the attempt that very night. I softly opened the door of the room in which the girls were sleeping and drew the keys out of the pocket of her coat hanging on the back of the door.

In the half-light from the door, I looked at the two children lying peacefully together in the big bed. When the girl was asleep the frown that had now become almost permanent during the day dissolved, and she looked younger than her years and completely innocent.

Since it was too late for the trams, I walked all the way to the girl's house and found my way round to the back of the garden. I managed to get over the low wall that surrounded it and cautiously advanced to the rear of the house. To my profound disappointment, the door was as securely boarded up as the front-door. It would take a long time with a hammer and crowbar to get through and the noise would alert the neighbours within a few minutes.

I immediately retraced my steps. I had more difficulty getting over the wall from the garden-side because the ground was lower and so the wall was higher. In scrabbling onto the top, I made some noise and saw—or thought I saw—a light come on above the coach-house. There must be a dwelling up there. Had someone heard me and turned on a light? I froze and waited. Nothing happened. I couldn't even be sure of what I had seen, and it might have been the way the moon's reflection caught a glass-pane. After a minute or two I lowered myself over the wall onto the path and crept back to the street.

I didn't know if it was just my imagination, but as I walked home I kept thinking I heard footsteps behind me. When I stopped, they stopped. If I looked back I could not be sure the street behind me was empty because the inadequacy of the wartime street-lighting left it in darkness. Had someone followed me from the house? Had my climb over the wall awoken someone in the coach-house? Or was I hearing merely the echo of my own steps?

In bed an hour or so later and unable to get to sleep, I wondered if the girl had been lying and did in fact know the combination that would open the safe. She just did not trust me with its contents, and that's why she had denied knowing it.

I decided I did not dare ask her if there was an apartment above the coach-house because I did not want her to know of my attempt to enter the house. Given her unnatural interest in money, she was quite capable of accusing me of trying to appropriate it for myself when the truth was that I had taken a huge risk in order to benefit her.

* * *

I slept late the next morning and then was awakened by my wife shaking me and telling me the girl was in a terrible state because her keys had vanished.

How could I have been so stupid? I who had always taken such pride in being meticulous about every detail? The truth was that I was so upset and exhausted when I came in that I had forgotten to replace the keys.

I dressed and hurried into the living-room. The girl instantly screamed at me: *You took them, didn't you? You thought you could get Daddy's money.*

I could think of nothing better to say than that I had found them last night on the floor in the hall and had put them in my pocket to give back to her. She snatched them from me and said: *That's a lie. They were in my pocket when I went to bed last night. I know you want to steal from Daddy. That's why you asked me all those questions about the safe and the house.* Then she ran into her room.

My daughters were furious with the girl and denounced her behaviour as ungrateful and malicious. Neither of them had any reason to suppose that I had indeed taken the keys.

I had now given up all hope of raising enough money for the bribe, but I still thought it might be possible to get the girl back into the system.

* * *

That evening something happened that seemed at the time to offer the possibility of a solution. I should explain that the only relatives either my wife or I had in the city were connections by marriage. They were my brother-in-law and his wife. I always called him my 'brother-in-law' for the sake of simplicity, but the truth is that he was my sister's husband's brother. My sister and her husband still lived in the former capital, where she and I had grown up, but my brother-in-law and his wife had come to the city five years earlier for the sake of his work as a doctor in a hospital, and the four of us had become quite good friends. His wife had been brought up in the city and in fact her mother—though not her father—was from the same community as the girl. They had two children of roughly the same age as our girls, and so we did family things together now and then.

When my brother-in-law ended his visit, I offered to accompany him to the tram-stop.

As we were going down the stairs, we met the joiner's wife as she was letting herself into her apartment. She smiled and said: *I saw your little girl and your wife's niece earlier. They did make a sweet pair.*

I said: *We call her that but she's not our niece exactly. She's the daughter of a cousin of mine.*

As we walked on down the stairs, my brother-in-law looked at me quizzically. We had told him the girl was just a friend of our daughter, and of course he knew she was not my cousin's daughter since he had met that young woman several times.

On an impulse I decided to tell him the truth. For one thing I had an urge to share it with someone—and someone who was more or less a member of the family and therefore, I believed, completely trustworthy. Another motive was that, since his wife was half a member of the girl's community, I thought he might be able to help me to get some assistance from it.

I told him the whole story very quietly as we walked slowly towards his tram-stop. He said little except for the strange remark that he wished I hadn't told him. I asked him to tell nobody except his wife but to try to find out if there was any means by which responsibility for the girl could be lifted from our shoulders by her own community.

* * *

When we listened to the evening news the following night, all of us realised that things had become more serious. The authorities had announced yet another order relating to the aliens: the Enemy's own laws on 'ethnic hygiene' which already applied in that country were being enacted in our nation and would be effective from exactly one week later.

Among other stipulations, it meant that all members of the 'protected community' of all ages were required to wear a prominent badge in public. To accompany that, there would be a considerable increase in the number of random checks on identity-cards in the street, and anyone found without a badge carrying an identity-card that indicated the bearer was required to have one, would be arrested. The authorities claimed that the community had been a parasitic presence in our nation for many centuries and was allowed to live among us only on sufferance and that the patient forbearance of our people was coming to an end.

My wife and I exchanged a look. If the girl was stopped in the street, the surname on her identity-card would betray her membership of the community and reveal that she had not registered, and of course she would not be wearing the badge.

We said nothing until the girls were in bed. My wife then told me how worried she was that we were breaking the law. I told her that once the girl's parents had returned to the city, they would take over responsibility for her, and it would be their task to get the girl back into the system.

The girl did not look very typical of her community, but my wife was worried she might be detected by a random check. I said we'd keep her at home for the first few days and see how many such inspections were being made in our part of the town.

My wife was afraid that if she was caught by one, we might have to pay a fine for not having registered her and wondered if her parents would pay it for us. I tried to reassure her on that point and said that anyway, there was no reason to suppose the authorities were even aware of the girl's existence and if they were, they had no reason to suppose she was not with her parents.

But would the parents ever return? I thought about the fact that the laws on 'ethnic hygiene' had already been applied in the occupying power's own territory. This meant that the parents, in what was the capital during the invasion, had been subject to them as soon as the Western Zone was annexed. In our country we were at the beginning of a process which was either well advanced or even completed in the Enemy's own territory.

* * *

That Friday afternoon I took the girl to the café alone in order to save money. Again, she was watching the door like a pointer all the time and was unwilling to leave at six. I did not see the proprietor this time.

Perhaps because I was so nervous, I noticed that among the numerous groups of people—mostly couples or families with children—who were sitting at the tables around us, there was a man seated alone who appeared to be taking an interest in myself and the girl. Whenever my gaze fell on him his head was turned towards us, and then he would look away.

* * *

A week after the announcement, the laws on 'ethnic hygiene' came into force. We kept the girl at home for three days—three days of boredom and short temper on her part. During that time I walked around the city and took long tram-rides on unfamiliar routes. What I discovered was that while the normal police and the auxiliary police were examining the identity-cards of people in the centre—both those wearing badges and those without—there seemed to be no or very few checks outside that area. I saw none at all in our neighbourhood.

* * *

The day after the regulations took effect, my brother-in-law called on us late in the evening. He told me he had asked his wife to use her connections with the girl's community to find out about her family and see if anyone would take responsibility for her. He had very discouraging news and said: *Because of who her father is and what he has done, nobody wants to get involved with her.*

I was astonished and said: *They hate the father so much that they won't help his child?*

He said: *No, it's not that. They are sorry for the girl but they are literally frightened to help her.*

I pressed him about the reasons for that attitude, and he told me precisely what his wife had learned, and we went over the words again and again to see what meaning we could extract from them. All she had been told was that the father cheated the wrong people over the store. He said people were frightened to tell her any more than that.

His visit left me in a state of deep alarm. Why should anyone be afraid to help the girl? And did it mean that by taking her in I had brought on myself and my family a further danger in addition to the one that I knew about?

I felt I had run out of options. And now it came to me that in my panic-stricken haste to find a solution, I had failed to think ahead. Even if I had managed to get the girl back into the system, where would she go now that her house was sealed, she had no other relatives, and her own community was unwilling to help her?

* * *

I kept thinking about what my brother-in-law had told me: the father cheated the wrong people over the store.

Everything came together. All the things I had tried not to notice. The man had made powerful enemies inside his community. He had come from outside the city and had obtained ownership or part-ownership of its biggest department store. In doing so he had presumably used dubious methods—perhaps fraud, or perhaps intimidation. I knew there were gangsters inside the Old City who practised protection rackets and controlled prostitution and gambling. These men, believing that he owed them money or convinced that he had cheated them, might have threatened to kidnap or otherwise harm the girl. This would explain why it was not thought to be safe for anyone to shelter her.

The thug I had spoken to at the store was not an employee of the girl's father but one of the men who had seized control of the business from him. Everyone knew he was ruined and that was why they were calling in loans. The fact that he was bankrupt was why he was not sending his daughter to an expensive school. And the reason why the other girls from her community shunned her at school was that they all knew about her father.

Everything I had hoped for was illusory: the prospect of a job, even of being reimbursed for my expenses. That was what I now assumed. At this point I gave up keeping the schedule of costs incurred on the girl's behalf.

* * *

By the fourth day it seemed safe to let the girl go to neighbouring shops, cafés, and parks, and so my wife took her out that morning.

That was good, but when I bought the evening paper to read over my lunch, I found a new regulation had come into force that day with immediate effect: anyone wearing the badge would not be allowed into public buildings, into cafés or restaurants, or on buses or trams.

When I got home my wife took me aside and said there had been no problems with checks on identity-cards, but that as she and the girl were coming back for lunch, the concierge had given them a malign smile and remarked as if to herself: *I wonder if we've forgotten something.*

This was very alarming. We both interpreted it to mean that the girl should be wearing a badge. Our one comfort was that she had no evidence—as far as we knew—that the girl belonged to the community. Without that, she would surely not risk reporting the matter to the police because she must realise that if her suspicions were unfounded, she would not only annoy the authorities but irritate all the occupants of the other apartments on whom she relied for tips and various other favours.

* * *

The following afternoon the two younger girls went out to buy something just before we had supper. My wife and other daughter and I began to discuss the morality of the new laws on 'ethnic hygiene'. My wife and I talked of how stupid and nasty they were, but my daughter disagreed and said: *It seems to me that different kinds of people need to stay within their own groups. The mixing of blood is not a good idea.* I said that might be true of dogs or cattle but not human beings. I wondered who had been putting such ideas into her head. I was horrified that a child of mine would express such sentiments. And it occurred to me that if she really believed those things, she was likely to prove an obstacle to the resolution of our problem.

* * *

The next day was a Friday, and my wife and I discussed in private whether to let the girl go to the café since it was in the city-centre. We decided that the probability of an inspection of identity-cards was relatively low since I had seen very few, and so the girl and I took the tram and got there at five. When we came in, the proprietor looked at us without smiling. Of course, he knew the girl was not wearing the badge as she should have been. In that moment it suddenly struck me that our visit was pointless since her parents—assuming they were wearing the badge—would not be allowed into the café anyway.

I insisted we stay no longer than the bare minimum. When we rose to leave the proprietor hurried forward and drew me out of earshot of the girl. In a low voice he asked me not to bring her again because he didn't want any trouble. He seemed genuinely embarrassed and apologetic.

As we were waiting at the tram-stop, two members of the auxiliary police came along. To my dismay they stopped and asked us for our identity-cards. I had anticipated this eventuality, and my wife and I had prepared a response. I handed my card over but with a glance at the girl I said with a smile: *My daughter has just told me that she has left her card at home, the foolish child.*

One of the men copied my name and address into his notebook and asked for the girl's name. I gave that of my younger daughter, which was what I had previously decided to do in such an emergency. They told me my daughter would have to report to the local police-station by noon tomorrow with her card and walked on. My heart was thumping, and when they had got some paces away I had a sort of nervous reaction in which the terror I had been holding at bay overwhelmed me. For several minutes I was struggling for breath and could not speak. The girl, in contrast, seemed completely unaffected, and I felt a strong sense of anger towards her—irrationally, as I knew even at the time. She could hardly be blamed for failing to realise how much danger we had been in—even though it was because of her.

I could not avoid telling my wife, and she was angry and upset at what had happened and at the fact that my action had implicated my younger daughter.

I told the girl we would not return to the café next week, and she threw a tantrum. I had to promise to go there every Friday in case any of her family appeared—though I knew that was not going to happen. And I had to agree to pass her house at least once a week to make sure that one of the café's cards was still visible. In fact, I had decided it was too dangerous to go back to the café even alone since the proprietor knew of my connection with the girl, and if enquiries had led the authorities to him—which was perfectly possible since several people probably knew of the family's visits there—he could tell them that I came there late on Friday afternoons.

* * *

The next morning I gave my younger daughter instructions and then accompanied her to the police-station in our district, where all she was required to do was to show them her identity-card. It was endorsed with a stamp saying the holder had been warned for failing to carry it and a further offence would be punished.

As I walked her to her tram-stop, I found I couldn't speak and my eyes were filling with tears at the thought of what I had exposed my beloved child to. Suppose one of the officers who had stopped us yesterday had happened to be in the station and had noticed that the girl was not the one he had seen the previous day? By impersonating the girl she had committed an offence which, if discovered, could have resulted in very serious punishment for both of us. It was one thing to risk that for oneself, but for a parent to have put his child in that position was deeply shaming.

For the next few days, we dared not let the girl leave the apartment even for the comparatively safe streets of our district. With that stamp in our daughter's identity-card, we could not use the same trick again.

* * *

I was walking from the office towards my tram-stop one day when I met a woman who had been employed in another section of my department. Because her work-place was near mine we had chatted occasionally, but she had been dismissed when the new regulations came into force because she had been unable to produce the required proof of an exclusively Christian heritage. We now talked for a while, and she showed me her new identity-card. It had a big

yellow symbol on the cover, and when she showed me the page with
her photograph I noticed that instead of referring to the bearer as
a citizen, as all identity-cards had hitherto done, it described her
as 'an alien residing in the country by virtue of the goodwill of the
national population'.

* * *

The next time I passed the girl's house I almost failed to notice that
the original poster had been covered by a new one which looked
almost identical. The wording, however, was significantly different:
*Following the relocation of the original occupier, this property has been
restored to the ownership of the nation.*

Perhaps unwisely—but I couldn't bear to deceive my wife—I
told her that I was now sure that the girl's father was not wealthy
and that he was not going to return.

She told our elder child, and her response was impulsive and
I'm sure she didn't mean it: she said we should get rid of the girl,
even if that meant just taking her to another part of the city and
abandoning her. I refused and pointed out that she would be picked
up by the authorities and would lead them straight back to us.

* * *

About now something I had foreseen happened. It was announced
that the laws of ethnic hygiene were being tightened. From this
point onwards, anyone without all four grandparents of what was
called 'ethnic acceptability' suffered the civil penalties of those who
had only two or fewer grandparents meeting the required criteria.
Moreover, anyone married to someone in that category would suffer the same sanctions. I instantly thought of my brother-in-law.
His wife was now in the 'unacceptable' category and so was he since
a spouse, even with the required certificate of 'ethnic acceptability',
suffered the same penalties as the person to whom he or she was
married. Since he was a public employee, that would mean dismissal from his post with loss of pension rights.

* * *

Then one afternoon as I came into the building with my elder daughter, I passed the concierge's son lounging against the wall with a couple of men who were wearing the uniform of the auxiliary police. They all stared at me in a boorish manner without returning my greeting.

That was a worrying development. If one of those thugs happened to be present when the concierge demanded to see the girl's identity-card, it might be impossible to resist.

There was something else that I was worried about. I didn't at all like the way the young lout looked at my daughter.

* * *

On the very day we had agreed to allow the girl out again provided she stayed close to the apartment, the wireless announced at breakfast that yet another regulation was about to come into effect. This one required that the concierge in apartment buildings note all comings and goings of tenants and their visitors, and it gave him or her the authority to check the identity-card of all non-residents. We all stared at each other in horror. The regulation came into effect in precisely two weeks. We had no time to discuss its implications before the three of us had to hurry off to catch our trams, but they were obviously ominous.

As we passed the concierge's hatch she popped out and gave me a thin-lipped smile of triumph. I managed to smile back at the evil old crow and to say: *In two weeks you will have your desire and be able to examine all the identity-cards you wish to.* I said that in order to give the impression of breezy unconcern.

She said: *How is your wife's little niece, or perhaps I should say your little niece? Or your cousin or whatever it is this week. I never see her leave the apartment. Is she still there? Is she unwell?*

I said: *She has been a little unwell. Thank you for your solicitude.*

As I travelled to the office I asked myself: Could an identity-card be bought on the black market? Could one be forged in the name of my cousin's daughter? Could the girl's identity-card—which was no longer valid since it showed she was over fourteen and which, because of the revealing surname, was very dangerous—be changed by forgery into an acceptable one?

One option I ruled out was returning to my former colleague and accepting his terms for getting her registration legitimised. Something that had been at the back of my mind now came to the forefront. During the three weeks following my meeting with him, I thought I saw him several times—twice in the street and once in a restaurant. On this very day I saw him again near my office and he looked at me—as he had not done on the previous three occasions—and made a grimace with his face that I took for a malevolent smile. How strange that having not seen him for a couple of years, I now kept glimpsing him. I could not stop myself wondering if he was following me. What did that leer mean? Was he inviting me to offer him the bribe? Was he commiserating with me after guessing that it was I and not some friend of mine who needed help? Was he threatening me? Or was he warning me of some danger which he knew of but I did not? Since he was working in the Department of Protection, I wondered if he had some idea of what was being planned for the 'protected community'.

* * *

That evening there was yet another new announcement on the wireless. No member of the minority community was henceforth allowed to own a business of any kind or any real estate outside the Old City. All such assets would be confiscated by the authorities and sold to those with proof of citizenship. I had foreseen that, since it was the logical culmination of the vast process of accounting for assets that my department had been engaged upon. I realised it would hugely increase our workload.

* * *

Later that night my wife and I discussed the consequences of the new regulation about identity-cards. It meant we would have to keep the girl in the apartment all day, and she would be able to leave only at night when the concierge was asleep—and even that would be risky since she might choose to stay awake in order to check on us. And the girl would have to carry our younger daughter's identity-card if she did ever get past the evil old woman and manage to go out. Moreover, since there would be few people about at night, the risk of her being checked would be high and the impersonation might be spotted.

Her health would assuredly suffer without either exercise or daylight. We had somehow to find a solution to the problem, and we had less than two weeks.

For some time it had happened that I would occasionally wake in the middle of the night and find my wife crying quietly beside me halfway between sleeping and waking. I had at first wondered whether to speak and try to comfort her, but I hadn't done so. As the weeks passed, I found myself becoming less sympathetic and actually angry at her weakness and self-indulgence. Yet even at the time I knew that what was upsetting me was not her misery but my own sense of guilt.

* * *

The next afternoon I happened to overtake my elder daughter coming back from her tram-stop. As we entered our building, I saw that the concierge's son was again hanging around the entrance with two of his auxiliary police friends. I went up the stairs but realised that my daughter had stopped to talk to them. I waited, but she did not look at me and seemed engrossed in her conversation. I continued up to our apartment. When she came in a few minutes later, I asked her what she thought she was doing paying any attention to a ruffian like that. She said she had talked to him a few times and he was more intelligent and pleasanter than I realised. She accused me of being a snob.

I hesitated to tell her not to speak to him again because it occurred to me that if she suddenly snubbed him, it would annoy him and increase the likelihood of his making trouble for us. Besides, I suspected she would not obey me.

My wife agreed with me later that night that our daughter showed signs of rebelling against the values and traditions we had taught her. For several weeks she had been making remarks about being nothing more than a downtrodden worker now that she was slaving for a pittance in a low-skilled job. And on several occasions she had sneered at us and her sister for what she called our 'bourgeois assumptions'.

* * *

Our lives were being dramatically changed because of the presence of the girl. Almost without making a conscious decision, we had taken measures to hide her existence from people who came to the apartment. We had asked her not to answer the door if anyone knocked but instead to go to her room—at least until we knew who it was. We had started to discourage unannounced visits and had virtually stopped inviting people to our home. As a result, we found ourselves being asked out less and less often. That was only partly because of the privations of the wartime situation, which meant everyone found it difficult to offer hospitality. My wife and I accepted our increasingly restricted lives with resignation, but our daughters resented it and blamed it on the girl.

I calculated that by now the real value of my salary had dropped to half of what it was before the War began. And that did not take into account the extra expenses incurred in feeding and clothing the girl. The measures we had to take to save money were having a greater and greater impact on our lives. I often walked back from work to avoid paying the tram-fare. And since the number of trams had been reduced, it was often not much slower than waiting for one.

It was hard to blame my daughters for wishing the girl was out of the apartment, but I did try to stop them making their feelings known to her. Yet when they made such remarks to her face she fought back fiercely and would tell them how much she loathed being in our 'tiny cramped little hovel' and eating our 'nasty badly-cooked mess'. Sometimes my wife and I would begin by defending her against our own children until her contempt for all of us became so offensive that we would round on her, and then the argument would end with her throwing a tantrum and uttering a tirade of insults after which she would run to her room.

Perhaps she should stay there the whole time, my elder daughter remarked after one such scene.

Her sister endorsed that in the most heartfelt terms.

How bitterly I wished I had paid the bribe that my former colleague demanded. If I had, the problem would have been solved by now.

* * *

Things were steadily getting more difficult for members of the girl's community and even for people who did not regard themselves as belonging to it, but whose affiliation was now revealed on their identity-card. My head of section had seen the implications of the rules on 'ethnic hygiene' and had started threatening certain people with this argument: *You are one-quarter alien but we can overlook that if you tell us where your fully alien cousins are hiding.*

I could not stop worrying that if such pressure were applied to my brother-in-law over his wife and children, he might be forced to reveal I was concealing an unregistered member of that community. Not having heard from him for a few weeks, I decided to ring him from my office at his place of work. The colleague who answered the telephone at the hospital told me that my brother-in-law had been suspended 'while he sorted out his private life'. When I asked what that meant, he said his marriage had turned out to be an 'impediment to his career'.

I knew what he meant. I had heard of several cases where men who had married women who were wholly or partly alien were required to divorce them or face dismissal.

How ironic! I had confided in him only because his wife was compromised in that way but by doing so, I had put all of us in danger.

I decided it was not fair to keep from my wife the fact that I had told him about the girl and that he was now in trouble with the authorities.

Late that evening my wife and I sat in the living-room until one o'clock, and I told her what had happened with my brother-in-law. She was worried for his and his wife and children's sake but also saw the danger to ourselves. We agreed that we had to resolve the problem of the girl, and we discussed various options at considerable length.

In the end, we decided that our only remedy was to make a full and frank disclosure. I would go to the authorities and tell them the whole story: We had taken the girl in as an act of generosity to our daughter's schoolfriend long before there was any question of that being illegal.

We wondered if they would believe us if we told them we had no idea that she belonged to the community, and we agreed that was so implausible it would weaken our case. So we would tell them the truth: we had misunderstood the regulation and failed to register her for the new identity-card because of her birthday falling between the two dates.

She asked: *What do you think they will do?*

I said: *I suppose they'll fine me. Perhaps a couple of weeks' salary. Possibly a month's.*

She said: *Will it harm your position at work?*

Of course, I had kept from her the embarrassing incident with the file. I just said: *It might, but I can't see any other way to get out of the situation we're in.*

My wife said: *What will happen to the girl?*

I said: *I imagine she will be sent to join her family, and so it will be to her advantage.*

There was the irony: we were risking so much to keep the girl with us and yet, we thought, she herself would be better off if we revealed her presence to the authorities.

We had thirteen days before the concierge could demand to see the girl's identity-card. It was far better to own up before we were caught. We agreed that we would allow ourselves a couple of days to think it over, and then I would go to the authorities on the third day.

* * *

It was lucky—at least from one point of view—that we did decide to wait. For the next day all that we had resolved was thrown into doubt. I was leaving the office building at lunchtime when my former colleague came hurrying across the road from a café where I assume he had been waiting to see me come out. He thrust something at me and said: *Tell your friend about this.* Then he hurried away before I could speak.

What he had given me was a page from a newspaper published in the former capital and mainly circulated there. It was dated a few days ago, and there was a story in it about a man who had 'wilfully and in defiance of the laws on ethnic hygiene' concealed a child, the son of friends, who was a member of the 'protected community'. He had failed to register him and tried to pretend he was his own nephew. Fortunately a 'public-spirited' neighbour had informed the authorities. The paper reported that he had been fined a huge sum and sentenced to a year's detention in a labour camp.

This changed everything. A sentence of that kind would mean ruin, utter ruin, for my family. Confessing to the authorities was now out of the question.

But there was something else I had to think about. Why had my former colleague shown me the newspaper? Was he being generous and warning me of the risk that I—or 'my friend'—was running? Or was he trying to force me to pay for his help? Or just setting a price for keeping quiet? In that case if I failed to contact him would he, as another 'public-spirited' citizen, denounce me?

* * *

I could hardly wait for the girls to go to bed and leave my wife and myself alone that night. Eventually I was able to show the newspaper story to her. At first she was as horrified by it as I had been. But then she pointed out that its implications in relation to ourselves were not clear-cut. The man had been reported to the authorities whereas we were planning to come forward voluntarily. Moreover, the former capital—along with the rest of the Western Zone—was now constitutionally incorporated into the Enemy's country. Clearly the laws of ethnic hygiene were being more rigorously applied there than here. In short, she could not see any alternative to what we had agreed to do: confess to the authorities.

Finally I had to tell her that I had kept something back. The situation was more serious than she knew because of the incident with the file which I now related to her. My previous 'offence' was in my record and would be used against me. This meant that, even taking into account the mitigating facts she had identified, I would certainly be dismissed at the very least.

She said she understood, but in that case, what could we do? In a few days the concierge would be able to bring the police down upon us.

I said we would have to conceal the girl's presence in the apartment. She would stay in it day and night and be hidden from all visitors. My wife was horrified. There were many objections. If we took this step, we would be burdened with the girl for the foreseeable future. It would be hard to conceal from the neighbours that she was there. It would be unkind and even dangerous to the girl herself not to allow her any fresh air or daylight or exercise. It was unfair on our daughters to take the risk involved.

We grew heated but were having to conduct our argument in low voices since the girls were on the other side of the wall.

I conceded all those points but maintained that we had no alternative. There was no way to hand the girl in to the authorities without incriminating ourselves. We had already passed the point of no return, and from now on our fate was tied to hers. All we could do now was to wait for her parents to claim her.

How? my wife demanded. *How would they find her?*

She was making a valid point. The one tenuous thread that would lead the parents to their child was the card—or cards—from the café pinned to the door of their house. But that meant someone had to go to the café every Friday at five and wait for the parents to register their presence in some manner because they would not legally be allowed in.

The proprietor would recognise me from my three visits and, now that the screw was tightening, might be tempted to report me to the authorities because of my link with the girl. All of which meant I could not go. My wife had accompanied us only on the first occasion, and the chances were that the owner would not remember her. And so we agreed she would have to make those regular visits. She would have to recognise any one of the girl's family who might appear at the door or the window just from her memory of the photograph that the girl had destroyed. And in order to avert the proprietor's suspicion, she could not turn up only at five on Fridays but would have to drop in at other times during the week. (I thought with dismay of the expense. One cup of coffee there would pay for an entire family meal at home.)

This still left the problem that the concierge knew the girl was living with us and was waiting for the moment—only ten days away—when she could demand to look at her identity-card. Not only would she find that it was now invalid, but she would almost certainly recognise the surname as incriminating. We could not see how to get around that obstacle.

Moreover, at any moment my brother-in-law, under pressure and with his career at stake, might give in to the temptation to tell the authorities about us. There was nothing we could do about that. As my wife said, we just had to hope he would go through with the divorce and that would be the end of the matter. We decided not to get in touch with him but wait for him to tell us what was happening.

Unable to sleep that night, I found my thoughts going round and round the same scenes. And now it occurred to me that if a newspaper could cross the border, so could a letter. Had the parents written by now? I could not see any means of finding out if a letter to the girl had been delivered to her house. Although I was aware it would not serve any purpose, I decided I would walk past it in the next day or two.

The next day my head of section was arrested. When I heard it, I was terrified. I assumed the charge was stealing and embezzlement and was afraid I would somehow be sucked into the affair if the facts of what had been going on came to light. However, it emerged that he, like the director, had been ensnared by his own deputy's machinations, and the offence was one that involved only himself.

I wasn't sure whether to be pleased at the downfall of this brutal and corrupt man or horrified that life was now so irrational that even someone as ruthlessly self-serving as he was no longer safe.

* * *

The following evening on leaving work I took the tram out to the fashionable district and walked past the girl's house on the opposite side of the street. I barely slowed as I reached it. Nothing seemed to have changed. The boards were still across the door and the cards from the café were still nailed to them—faded and tattered by the weather but still perfectly recognisable. I was quickening my pace when I saw the friendly maid from next door smiling at me. I crossed to speak to her.

She asked me if I knew the family at the house I was taking an interest in. It sounded like an innocent question with no hidden motives, but I hesitated. Why should she assume I was interested in that house? Was she trying to entrap me? I said I knew who the head of the family was but had never met him.

Then she told me that about four days ago, the authorities came and banged on the doors of all the neighbours and told them they were looking for the daughter of the family who had lived in that house. They could account for the rest of the household, they said, but the girl had gone missing.

I nodded as she spoke and tried to give the impression that this was a mildly interesting story of no personal concern to myself.

Nobody, the woman said, *had any idea where the girl was, and nobody had seen her for several months.*

That was both reassuring—the police had been told nothing that led to myself—and deeply alarming: they were after all making a strenuous effort to find her.

The woman said: *The poor little mite. I wonder what has happened to her. Her parents are trapped in the capital with the little boy and her elder brother is in a prisoner-of-war camp somewhere.*

I said: *That's a sad story. Have none of her relatives come looking for her?*

She shook her head. She was beginning to look a little suspicious herself, and that encouraged me to trust her. If she feared I was trying to compromise her, that suggested she felt she could be entrapped, and that must be because her sympathies lay on the right side.

I smiled and said: *I suppose you would know if any of them did come back?*

She seemed to be reassured by my question and said: *Oh yes, they'd be sure to come and ask me. I was always friendly with them—especially the little girl.*

I felt a sense of relief. She had surely not noticed the girl getting out of the taxi on the last occasion I had brought her or she would have mentioned it.

She added: *Of course, they wouldn't be able to get in since it's no longer their property.*

I said: *I pass this way now and then and this is such an engaging story that I'll ask you what happens, if I see you. As I said, I just know who the family are because I go into their store occasionally.*

She nodded and said: *Do you think any of them will ever come back?*

I shrugged and we parted. At least I now had a means of knowing if any of the family did return.

I became tormented by my uncertainty over what the authorities knew or could establish about the chain of links that associated us with the girl. I went through all the connections, hoping that each of them had been dissolved. I remembered it had only been a few months ago that the two girls had gone to school and come home together. But that had not lasted long. Would anybody at the school now remember their brief friendship?

* * *

At supper that evening, my elder daughter seemed bent on provoking an argument with myself and her mother. She started saying that the future lay in collaborating with the occupying power and not in pretending our national sovereignty was going to be miraculously restored to us. *Who is going to fight for our freedom?* she demanded sarcastically. *We failed to do it for ourselves and now it's too late. Any nation that conquered the Enemy would just replace one foreign regime with another and it would be a worse one. The Enemy has given us peace and security from attack and in allowing us a government of our own people—a privilege they have not granted to some other defeated countries—they have left us a large degree of freedom provided we do not overstep the mark. We should learn to be satisfied with that.*

I knew she was trying to justify her relationship with the thuggish son of the concierge, and I felt she was trying to convince herself as much as us. My wife and I failed to rise to the bait and the younger girls showed no interest in the conversation. But it was worrying— particularly in the light of what we were about to announce—that my daughter appeared to be falling under the influence of the concierge's son and his friends. In the last few days she had often stopped in the hallway for long periods to chat and joke with them.

When my wife and I were alone I told her what I had learned from the friendly maid: that the girl's parents and younger brother were still trapped in the former capital. I wondered if we should tell her that. (I did not say I had no reason to suppose the maid was correct.)

My wife said: *Yes, of course. It will cheer her up. It's cheered me up to know they are safe and might soon return to take her off our hands.*

I said: *I don't think it's as straightforward as that. The Enemy has a grudge against that community and wants to squeeze as much of their wealth out of them as possible. It might not be such good news.*

She accepted that and so we decided to keep this piece of information from the girl–though it meant leaving her in a state of uncertainty, which carried its own risks.

Our elder daughter came home the next evening and told us she had been dismissed. What had happened was this: While the owner was out of the shop, the other girl who worked there, the 'favourite', had been even ruder and more overbearing than usual and my daughter had defended herself. There had been an argument and in the middle of it, the owner had come back and, without listening to my daughter's side of it, had sacked her on the spot.

* * *

The War was getting closer. The Enemy was losing and its population was suffering heavy air-raids which was encouraging, but that meant conditions were worsening for us as well. As the regulations about rationing became increasingly stringent, we grew hungrier and hungrier. Sometimes a fleet of aircraft passed overhead on their way to drop bombs on other cities. Now and then one fell on ours, and I saw it as a foretaste of what was to come. Civil society was breaking down under the arbitrary arrests, the bullying of the auxiliary police, and the forced conscription of young men into the armed services of the Enemy. In our city alone, there must have been hundreds if not thousands of people hiding with their families or in empty apartments or abandoned warehouses.

The square in front of the cathedral where the public-executions took place often had five or six bodies hanging from lamp-posts. I avoided the place but the first time I saw a body, it had a placard around its neck: *He hid an enemy of our people.*

Stray dogs had become a serious problem—even a danger. So many people had left suddenly and for one reason or another had neither taken their dogs with them nor had them destroyed, that there were thousands of them roaming the streets looking for food. They often formed packs and those could be very dangerous.

* * *

My wife and I had agreed we had to inform the three youngsters of what we had decided about hiding the girl. We had to tell them everything so they would understand how little choice we had and how important it was that nobody found out she was in the apartment. So after supper the next evening we stayed sitting round the table, and I outlined the plight we were now in.

There were a few things I didn't tell them: how severely the man in the capital had been punished for hiding a child, my problems at work over the file, and my worries about both my former colleague and my brother-in-law. I explained the difficulty now was that the girl could neither leave since she had nowhere to go nor stay since the concierge knew she was in the apartment, and even if she was not seen, the nasty old creature would sooner or later inform the authorities.

It was my younger daughter—the bright little thing—who came up with an idea. Her act of impersonation at the police-station had prompted it, she explained. What we should do was to stage a performance to make the concierge believe the girl had gone. She herself would pretend to be her and, since they were the same height and build, it had a good chance of success. Just before the deception, she would cut her own dark hair as short as the girl's and dye it the same shade of blonde.

We all objected that the concierge would not be taken in. She had seen and talked to both girls often enough to be able to distinguish them.

My daughter had taken account of that and said we needed to find a time when she would not be there.

I asked: *In that case, why would she believe that the girl had left?*

Because, my daughter explained, *we would stage a scene that would be witnessed by neighbours who would tell her that they had seen the girl depart. Why would it occur to her that they were mistaken?*

I think none of the three adults were confident it would suc-
ceed, but it seemed to be our best chance. The two younger girls saw
it as a game and were excited at the prospect.

We now had to find out if the concierge went out at the same
time every day or—less conveniently—every week so her absence
could be predicted. Each of us had noticed her getting into or out
of a taxi a few times, and we all tried to remember whether it was
on the same day. We felt it was always at the end of the week—a
Thursday or a Friday—and in the afternoon. I had a vague memory
that on at least one of the Fridays I had been to the Viennese café,
I had noticed her coming home in a taxi just as I was arriving back.

My wife set the girl to watch at the window all day. By sitting
close to the glass and peering down it was possible to see someone
leaving the building, provided they moved far enough away from it
across the pavement. So she sat there hour after hour listening to
the wireless with her nose pressed to the pane.

My wife overcame her ingrained habit of reserve and started to
gossip with the neighbours at every opportunity.

I played my part by sitting through whole evenings in a café di-
agonally opposite our building from which I could see its entrance
and the windows of the concierge's apartment.

That occasioned something which gave me further cause for
alarm. On the third evening, I noticed a man in the café whom
I seemed to half-recognise. Was he the individual who had been
watching the girl and myself in the Viennese café? In that case, was
it just a coincidence that he was here? Or was he spying on me?

We now had nine days left before the concierge had the right to
demand anyone's identity-card, and that was a short space of time
to work out someone's pattern of behaviour—especially a weekly
cycle.

* * *

And then we had a stroke of luck. My wife picked up from a chatty
woman on the first floor—the clockmaker's wife—that every Friday

afternoon after lunch, the concierge went to visit her sister on the other side of the city and arrived back a couple of hours later. The next day was a Friday, and the girl and my wife watched through the window. Sure enough, a taxi pulled up shortly after two o'clock, and the concierge boarded it.

She returned late in the afternoon. For all that time her hatch remained closed and dark.

The following Friday would have to be the day on which we carried out our charade. It was cutting it fine since the regulation giving her the right to demand an identity-card came into effect the day after that.

* * *

During the week-end my brother-in-law paid us a visit. He was deeply depressed as he told us that he and his wife had agreed a speedy divorce would be the best option. That way he would at least retain his post and therefore be able to pay for his wife—ex-wife, rather—and children to move into an apartment near his own.

When he had gone, my wife and I agreed that of course his family's situation was pitiable, but we admitted our relief that it looked as if there was no reason for him to be tempted to report our breach of the rules.

* * *

On Sunday evening, the nine o'clock news had yet another an-nouncement: No member of the 'protected community' was permitted to live anywhere inside the metropolitan district (which included a large rural area around the city) except the 'protected area' of the Old City. That rule would come into effect only one week from today. I listened in horror and out of the corner of my eye saw the girl's face remain impassive, as if she did not see what it meant. But my elder daughter remembered the girl's sneers at the poorer pupils who already lived there and said: *It seems you might have to lower yourself to go and live with your own kind.*

The girl stared at her as if she had not understood the words.

Late that night when we were going to bed, my wife pointed out that my brother-in-law's plans would be thwarted since his wife would have to move to the Old City with their children. It was worrying, but I told her that, by the same token, there was a chance we might be able to get the girl off our hands and into the Old City. I would look into it.

* * *

We had an unwelcome visitor a few days later. There was a knock at the door just after supper, and when I opened it I found our former domestic standing there with a nervous smile. Without thinking, I asked her to come in, and my wife and I entertained her in the sitting-room. It was odd to be sitting with her while my wife waited on her, bringing her a cup of coffee and a plate of cakes. The girl had, of course, hidden in her room when the doorbell went. I made an excuse to go to the kitchen but popped into the children's room and told her to stay there.

Our two daughters were perfectly happy to talk to the domestic—particularly the younger, who had always been a favourite of hers. The woman said she thought about all of us a great deal and had come merely to find out how we were in these 'troubled times'. After a while she asked where the girl was, and since I had been expecting that question, I instantly said that she had left us and gone back to her family.

To my relief she showed no further interest in the subject. It had struck me as soon as I saw her that she had come specifically to find out about the girl—perhaps having heard that there were rewards for turning in unregistered aliens. She had certainly been aware that the girl was a member of that community.

Later I wondered if she had merely dissembled her interest in the girl in order to avoid arousing our suspicions. I didn't think so, but it could not be ruled out.

She stayed only about forty minutes and said nothing about making a return visit.

* * *

On Tuesday afternoon, on the way home, I made a detour to the Old City and found that there were now only two entrances. The others had been sealed off by blocking streets with sturdy barriers and by bricking up doors. I stood at the eastern gate and watched as dozens of people arrived from other parts of the city or from the countryside. I saw the poor with their scanty belongings in a few battered suitcases, some pushing handcarts piled high with their possessions and often with chickens or ducks or rabbits in cages. And there were plenty of middle-class people getting out of taxis or being dropped off by friends with cars. As each passed the control-point, his or her identity-card was carefully scrutinised and compared with a list of names, and now and then some of them—including children—were made to stand aside for further checks. A few of those were taken away in the back of a police-van, a line of which was waiting nearby. It was clear to me that the girl would not be able to enter the Old City without it being discovered that her identity-card had not been renewed and, even more important, that the name on it revealed she was the daughter of a man of considerable interest to the authorities. They would want to know where she had been and who had been giving her shelter.

To bring her there and let her face that check-point would be to bring disaster down upon our own heads.

People were being allowed out of the Old City but only after going through another scrupulous check. I got close enough to listen, and the rule was that those who could prove they had legitimate employment which was considered to be useful to the state were permitted to leave as long as they returned by nine o'clock. All such employment for members of the 'protected community' was being phased out, however, and soon the only work that would be permitted would be inside the sealed perimeter.

That evening my wife mentioned at dinner that she had happened to pass the couturier where my daughter had worked, and it had shut down. When she asked at a nearby shop what had happened to the owner, she was told it had been raided a few days ago, and its owner and one of the staff had been taken away.

I looked at my elder daughter, but she continued to eat as if she had not heard her mother.

* * *

For some time there had been rumours about the planting of bombs in other cities and about similar terrorist acts of destruction in our city. So it was not a complete surprise when, the next day, there was an announcement on the evening news that had a dramatic effect on our lives—on the lives of everyone in the city, in fact. There would be a curfew with immediate effect. From eleven o'clock tomorrow night, nobody was to be out on the streets. There were no exceptions. Anyone found on the streets before six in the morning would be arrested or, if he or she tried to flee, shot on sight.

Also with immediate effect, there was to be a universal blackout in case of air-raids. At dusk the next day no street-lights would come on. Cars would be allowed only masked headlamps. No light could be shown by any private dwelling. To enforce that, a system of local wardens would be set up to patrol the streets looking for any chinks of light. Householders who contravened the rule would be severely punished.

Those were terrifying pieces of news. And yet at the same time they gave us a tiny thread of hope. If the authorities really believed there was a danger of the city being bombed, it implied the War was going against them very badly. And the introduction of the curfew suggested some sort of underground resistance was functioning.

What was certain was that our lives would become more inconvenient—perhaps more dangerous. We would be even less able to go out in the evening, given that we had to be safely home by eleven, and all trams, buses, and taxis would be off the road before that hour.

* * *

At last Friday came—the day on which we had to carry out the charade and the day before the regulation giving the concierge the right to demand an identity-card came into effect. And then disaster struck. When my wife went in to wake the younger girls, she found our daughter flushed and feverish. The doctor came later that morning and confirmed she had flu. Our plot depended on her, and so we had to postpone our plans for at least a week, thereby incurring the additional danger created by the new regulations.

My younger daughter could not be moved and had to have the bedroom to herself, so the girl was accommodated in that of my elder daughter. It was a small room, and she had only a mattress on the floor. This created friction since my elder daughter naturally resented the invasion of her privacy. Stuck in the apartment all day, the girl became bored and restless. Now that her attention was not to some extent absorbed by her relationship with my younger daughter, she became even more difficult and seemed constantly to be trying to provoke a quarrel. My elder daughter had never needed much provocation, and the temperature in the apartment rose.

* * *

To get away from the stifling atmosphere—a sick sister, a quarrelsome outsider, and two worried and I'm sure very irritating parents—my elder daughter started to spend even more time with the concierge's son during the course of this stressful week. On several occasions they went over the road to his favourite bar and passed the evening there. It seemed strange to me that she was fraternising with the son of the woman who had appointed herself our enemy and whose malign interest in us was putting us in so much danger.

Eventually when she came in late that Wednesday evening after everyone else had gone to bed, I raised it with her. She was very indignant and said that by befriending the young man she was helping to avert suspicion and also finding out what he and his mother knew about us. I asked what she had learned, and she said he had not mentioned the girl and she was certainly not going to raise the topic. I felt reassured by that, but I pointed out that she was setting a bad example for her younger sister by drinking in bars late at night and in the company of idle riff-raff and sleazy collaborationists. She flared up and said I was a snob and they were 'good lads' who had failed to find any other employment. And far from being collaborationists, they believed that working for the auxiliary police was a way of serving their country. Then she brought up the old theme: she had no desire to live up to the hopes and expectations of her parents and did not have the brains to do it even if she had wanted to. She told me I should place all my hopes of that kind on her younger sister, who would probably become a brilliant scholar or lawyer or something like that. She would be content if she could just run her own little dress business. Of course I told her I loved her and would love her whatever she did with her life, and it ended with both of us in tears hugging each other. All the time we had to keep our voices to a whisper to avoid waking the others.

Thinking over what she had said, I realised she was very unhappy. Her hopes of entering the world of *haute couture* had been thwarted by the War, what work she could find was not much more than slavery, and she had nothing to look forward to since even if— or when—the Occupation came to an end, what followed might be as bad or worse.

* * *

My younger child recovered after a few days, and when the following Friday arrived, we all knew what we had to do. The plan was this: My elder daughter and I would leave the building earlier than usual—at 7.45 instead of 8. At that time of day, the concierge was busy with breakfast. We hoped she would hear us passing and assume my younger daughter was with us. In fact, she would remain in the apartment. She would have trimmed her hair—already fairly short—and dyed it the previous day on getting back from school.

I would take the afternoon off work by feigning sickness. Just before getting home for lunch, I would order a taxi from the stand a few streets away and tell the driver—a man we had often used in more prosperous times and knew to be reliable—to come at half-past two precisely. I would emphasise the need for punctuality.

If I saw the concierge on the way in, as I hoped I would, I would mention that I had come back early to take my cousin's little daughter to the station, as she was going home. My wife would be accompanying her on the train and would stay with the child's family overnight and come back the next day.

To avoid the danger that the concierge might decide to cancel her weekly visit to her sister just for the sake of inspecting the girl's identity-card—which seemed unlikely—I would tell her that the girl was not leaving 'for a few hours' so she would assume she would be back in time to catch her.

That afternoon, the taxi would collect the concierge at around two if she kept to her usual routine. Not long after, as soon as the taxi I had ordered arrived, our younger child, looking as much like the girl as possible, would hurry down the stairs accompanied by my wife and myself carrying the suitcases. Anyone seeing our daughter would take her for the girl. If one of the neighbours tried to speak to her she would hold a handkerchief to her face and pretend to be weeping at the prospect of leaving us. She and my wife would get into the back of the taxi and make sure her face was not visible. I would deal with her luggage and also do something that I was dreading but accepted was necessary.

We needed to create some sort of scene in order to impress upon the memory of the neighbours the fact that the girl had driven off in a taxi. So I had agreed, very unwillingly, to provoke an argument with the taxi-driver.

I would angrily tell him he was late and we had agreed he would come at ten past two. He, poor man, would insist I was mistaken. I would have to raise my voice and shout at him—but

not so offensively that he refused the fare altogether, and to prevent that happening, my wife would take his side and yell at me.
The neighbours would certainly hear the row and look out of their
windows. We would then drive off and be dropped at the station.
We would pass through it and leave by another entrance where
there were taxis waiting. (We didn't want our driver to be able
to gossip about our odd change of plan.) One of them would
take us to a small boarding-house in a suburb on the other side
of the city that I had already visited to arrange a room. There my
wife and daughter would be left with the luggage. (One of the
suitcases would contain nothing but my wife's overnight things
and my daughter's school uniform. The other suitcase would be
empty and would be sacrificed for the sake of the deception, and
be thrown away by my wife.) My wife would stay there that night
but my daughter would wait for an hour during which she would
do her best to dye her hair back to its natural colour. It would be
shorter, of course, but not very noticeably so. She would put on
her school uniform, whose hat would cover her hair, and then set
off for home by tram.

About an hour after leaving the house, I would return as if I had
come back from the railway-station and then my younger daughter would get home at the normal time as if from school. My wife
would return the following afternoon and mention to neighbours
that she had escorted the child back to her parents' village.

* * *

We had examined the plan from every angle and believed we had
anticipated every eventuality. Of course, we were mistaken.

We did everything precisely as we had agreed: I came home,
ordering the taxi on the way and telling the concierge my cousin's
daughter was leaving later that afternoon. From our window we
watched the old woman get into her taxi and drive away, and when
ours arrived promptly at half-past two, we three hurried down the
stairs. However, the grille in front of the hatch was open, and as we

passed it the concierge's son called out to us: *Stop. I need to check that kid's identity-card.*

I gestured to my frightened wife and daughter to go on ahead as planned, and they hurried into the street and boarded the taxi.

The lout came scuttling out from his mother's apartment, but I blocked his way so he could not get to the street. I told him he was an impertinent oaf and had no authority to demand to see anyone's identity-card. He shouted that he was deputising for his mother and therefore had her powers under the new regulations. I laughed at that and told him he was talking nonsense. As we argued, the people in the other apartments on that floor opened their doors, and I heard the same happening above us. I loudly said that all the tenants in the building were potentially inconvenienced by his attempt to arrogate such power to himself, and I heard murmurs of approval from the others.

He threatened to call the police, and I decided to brazen it out and said: *You're welcome to bother them and bring them round here on a fool's errand, but I'm not going to let my cousin's daughter miss her train. And you have no power to stop us going.*

He stood with his great jaw hanging open, and I simply turned and hurried into the street. A moment later he came after me, but I jumped into the taxi and slammed and locked the door and told the driver to start. The churl grabbed the handle of the vehicle's door and peered in as it drove off.

My heart was thumping, and as the taxi turned the corner the three of us laughed with relief and hugged each other. At least I had not needed to stage an argument with the poor taxi-driver. The concierge would hear all about that scene as soon as she got home.

* * *

The rest of it went according to plan, but I could not help worrying about whether it had achieved its purpose and convinced the concierge and her son that the girl had left or whether it had actually had the opposite effect and aroused their suspicions.

The boor must have taken my daughter for the girl, or he would not have said he wanted to see her identity-card. And his mother would surely conclude that even if I had smuggled the girl out of the building because she had no valid identity-card, it was now too late to do anything about it.

One thing worried me. Was it possible that when the lout stared in through the window of the taxi he had caught a glimpse of my daughter and realised it was she and not the girl? In the confusion, had she been careful to keep her face hidden or had she looked out to watch the row? In that case he and his mother would guess that the girl was still in our apartment.

* * *

From now on it was essential that nobody other than the five of us have the slightest inkling that there was anyone but four family members in the apartment. That meant the girl had to stop playing the piano because she performed pieces that required so much more skill than my daughters possessed that it would have betrayed her presence. When I first told her that at lunch a couple of days before we put the deception into effect, she said tartly that she would try to play her pieces as badly as my daughters, and that did not go down at all well.

Unable to make music, she became more bored than ever—especially when she was alone in the apartment since at those times she could not listen to the wireless if there was supposed to be nobody there.

* * *

The next day I decided on a whim to pass the eastern entrance to the Old City again. I found it was sealed up completely. I walked all the way round to the western entrance and saw that, although it was still open, nobody was being allowed out. Its inhabitants were no longer permitted to work outside.

* * *

Dividing the rations for three adults and one child among four people was difficult. Both our daughters were going out every day, whereas the girl was staying at home. I was going to work, but I stinted myself. I ate hardly more than the girl even though I was almost twice her weight. My wife consumed the same as, or less than, the girl.

The tightening of rationing and the rise in prices led my wife to make a decision that must have been hard. The authorities had set up a system for dealing with orphaned and refugee children whose parents had been killed or otherwise incapacitated by the War. They advertised for unpaid helpers, and my wife volunteered to work three afternoons a week in return for her lunch and a snack in the afternoon 'off the ration-book'.

She started that work a day or two later, and some days that was all she ate so that the girl and I should share her rations.

* * *

There was something else that was worrying me, and this was a matter I was keeping from my wife. Two days after we had pretended she was escorting the girl back to her parents, the concierge accosted me as I was coming home from work and said: *How is the little girl—your wife's niece or whatever she is?*

As always I said: *You mean my cousin's daughter?* She smiled unnervingly. Then I explained: *She was fine when my wife left her yesterday. You remember, perhaps, that my wife took her back to her parents two days ago?*

The woman said: *Now isn't that interesting.*

It seemed an odd thing to say. She didn't explain her meaning. I just nodded and walked on up the stairs.

Then a couple of days later she stopped me and started a rambling conversation about the occupants of the apartment on the top floor of the neighbouring building. Eventually I began to see her drift. Her theme was that since their apartment, like mine, was twice as large as the others, those other tenants believed it was 'only right and proper' to give their concierge twice the tip that every other tenant gave her on the quarter-days when such gratuities were donated. Such a day was imminent.

I made some non-committal remark in response. I now had to decide whether to accept the hint. If she had guessed some of the truth, to give her a larger than usual tip would surely be to confirm her suspicions. On the other hand, to fail to give her what she wanted risked her making more trouble.

Eventually I decided I had to confide in my wife. When I did so that night, she horrified me by saying that the woman had been dropping the same sort of hints to her: mentioning the girl and then, as if the topic were related, bringing up the issue of her quarterly 'present'.

I was in favour of giving her not twice as much but a larger than usual tip on the grounds that if she were blackmailing us, she would not denounce us because then our donations would stop.

My wife loathed the idea of conceding that we were frightened of her and said that if we started on that course the demands would get larger and larger. Even assuming she was unaware of the identity of the girl's father and his significance to the authorities, the reward for betraying us for hiding any member of the girl's community was so large that the concierge would certainly denounce us if she was sure we were hiding an alien, and therefore it was better to call her bluff at this stage. She could have no real evidence and would surely be scared to summon the police to harass her most respectable tenants.

But did she have any evidence? I asked my wife if she thought the woman's son could have glimpsed our daughter's face either as she was hurrying past the hatch or when she was in the back of the taxi. She said she was absolutely certain that had not happened.

I suggested a compromise. Just as we were not sure if she was really extorting money from us because of her suspicions, we should give her an amount that would leave her unclear whether or not we were allowing ourselves to be blackmailed. I would give her an extra fifty per cent on top of the usual gratuity and tell her it was because her argument about the size of our apartment was a fair one.

My wife was still reluctant and pointed out how little we could afford to do that now—but she eventually consented.

So a short time later, on quarter-day, I handed the concierge the sum settled upon and explained that I had thought about what she had said and decided such an increase was just.

She took the money without any trace of pleasure or gratitude and just said: *It's up to you, sir.*

Now what did she mean by that? Was it merely that she was a little disappointed I had not doubled the amount? Or was it a menacing threat that if I chose not to satisfy her, I must take the consequences?

* * *

A few days later, the municipal administration published a manifest running to several pages which listed members of the 'protected community' whose whereabouts they were anxious to learn. Each was given a brief description. The name of the girl's father was not on it, but to my horror the girl herself was there. She was described in these terms: *Age 14. Slight build. Green eyes. Reddish-blonde hair worn short.* Beside each name was the size of the reward being offered. Most of them were the same amount, but to my surprise the bounty for the girl was among the largest. I realised the authorities must have thought she could lead them to her father's assets. But what did he own apart from the store or a share of it? I wondered if there was something else they were searching for: title-deeds or sight-drafts or account-numbers. If so, it was probably in the safe. Presumably they had no idea of its existence.

It struck me as strange that the authorities were so keen to find the girl when her father would have the information they wanted and he was in what was now part of the territory of the Enemy.

They must know that was where he was since his name did not appear on the index. With their mixture of microscopic thoroughness and overall lack of vision, had they lost track of him?

There was something else to worry about: the index was held in all public offices as well as post offices and libraries, and I feared the reward would encourage anyone who knew of the girl's tenuous links to my younger daughter and myself to investigate further.

* * *

My wife and I were now giving up a substantial portion of our rations to the girl, and our daughters resented the fact that we were going without so the girl could eat, and they were angered by her lack of gratitude. Everything about her now annoyed them: her idleness as she loafed about the apartment all day while they were out working or studying, her insolence towards her three elders, and her lack of interest in anything that did not directly affect her well-being. Now that she was alone three afternoons a week, she was getting more and more bored and restless.

* * *

The issue that was most preoccupying me, however, was not related to the girl but to my elder daughter. She was now going out drinking three or even four nights of the week with the concierge's son and his cronies in the auxiliary police. She often came home very late after spending time in his mother's apartment when the curfew closed the bars, and several times she returned more or less intoxicated. I always waited up for her and told her how disappointed by her conduct I was and that we would have to discuss it the next day. When we did, she was unrepentant and even surly. She said she now had more in common with those barely educated young men than with 'people like you and Mother'. When I asked her how she could afford to spend so much on drink or how the concierge's son could when he was unemployed, she said his friends had plenty of cash. I asked if she wasn't ashamed to be bought drinks by men who were collaborating with the occupying power, and she groaned and told me the world had changed and I had to realise you couldn't live in the past. There was nothing wrong with collaboration if it meant working together to make our country a better place, and there was a great deal our Enemy could teach us.

I could not help worrying about what my daughter might let slip when her tongue was loosened by alcohol. One hint to those licensed thugs, and we would all be in serious trouble. I did not discuss this with my wife, but eventually I realised she shared my concerns. She was as dismayed as I by our daughter's support for the people who were making money and advancing themselves through our nation's humiliation, but she had more insight than I into her motives. It was understandable, she said, that seeing her hopes of a career dashed by the War, she would attach herself to the faction that seemed to offer the prospect of advance and progress. Young people don't want to dwell on defeat and constraint but focus their energies and ambitions on something positive.

* * *

The evening after that conversation there was another announcement on the nine o'clock news. So far only members of the girl's community living in the metropolis and the administrative district surrounding it had been required to move into the 'protected area' of the Old City. To my astonishment, the wireless now announced that the rule was being extended to the whole province. It said: *The unhygienic and unsightly rural villages in which these people have generously been permitted to live, will be decontaminated and restored for the use of decent citizens of our nation. Their present occupants will be required to move into the 'protected area' of the Old City and live amongst their own people while they wait to be relocated. This regulation comes into effect at midnight tonight and all those affected by it must have complied within one week. Any who fail to obey will be dealt with in the harshest terms.* It made no sense. The numbers involved were enormous. There would not be space for them within the confines of the Old City. Moreover, the logistics of such an operation were formidable. This was yet another example of a massive bureaucratic blunder. I said nothing to any of my family but resolved to go the next afternoon and see what was happening.

* * *

It was only an hour later that there was another shock.

It had happened several times in the last few days that as I was going past her hatch, the concierge called out to me and said something that was either menacing or was an implied request for money. Once she said: *Would you like my lad to come up and do any small repairs for you, sir? He could use the money.* I declined the offer. Another time she beckoned me closer and in a loud whisper told me that if I ever had a guest whose identity-card I didn't want her to see, she could probably manage to be busy with something at the crucial moment. Then she added meaningfully: *Coming or going, sir. And man, woman, or child.* With a sly look she said: *I could be busy counting up my quarterly tips, though that wouldn't take me very long.*

I replied: *Thank you, but I don't think that will be required.*

Now, at about ten o'clock, there was a loud knock at the door. When the girl was out of sight in her room, I opened it and found the concierge's son looming up with a stupid grin on his face. He asked if there were any little jobs I would like him to do. I pretended to consider and then told him I could think of nothing.

I said: *Please don't ever come this late again. The children are usually in bed by now.*

The children? he repeated.

I realised my mistake. I said: *Both my daughters are my children.*

He gave me a half-witted smile and turned away.

It seemed ominous, and yet even after that, I could not be sure the concierge and her son knew anything for certain. I actually found myself longing for one of them to make an explicit threat. It would have made my course of action so much clearer.

* * *

The next afternoon I went to the western gate of the Old City and saw a scene of utter chaos. The square and the streets approaching it were crowded with people and carts and motor-vehicles. I could not get near the gate. I went into a café and asked if I could look out from their top floor. From up there I could just make out the gate with its checkpoint and I saw that, as I had expected, the policemen and soldiers on duty had abandoned any attempt to check the papers of those pressing to get in.

I hurried home and when my wife returned from her stint at the orphanage, I asked her to come into our bedroom. I told her what I had seen and said that this was a once-only opportunity to discharge ourselves of our responsibility for the girl without incurring any ill consequences. She would be able to walk into the Old City without her papers even being looked at and therefore nobody would notice that they were invalid and trace her back to us.

My wife leaped at this chance, and we talked about how it could be done. I would escort the girl, and we would have to risk breaking the curfew. I would take her out in the early hours of the next morning when the concierge was asleep. In order to avoid the patrols enforcing the curfew, we would take quiet back-streets to a shadowy place nearby. (I would have to reconnoitre to find one in the short time left before the curfew.) We would hide there for the rest of the night until the curfew ended at six and then make our way to the gate of the Old City which reopened at seven. We would have to watch it for perhaps another hour or so until it was again besieged by the press of people entering. Then the girl would join the throng crowding unchecked through the gate, and we would be rid of her at last.

Then my wife asked: *But will she agree?*

I said: *Why would she not choose to enter the protected area? And she will be among her own people again.*

I stressed that we had to act immediately. There was no certainty that the pressure of people would be maintained at this level, and once it slackened, the normal checks would resume.

My wife fetched the girl from the living room where the three young people were waiting for her to serve supper.

The girl sat on the bed and I told her that there was now a wonderful opportunity for her to join her own community in the Old City without any problem about her papers being checked. I explained the situation and described what I had seen.

To my dismay she refused to consider it. She said: *You want to get rid of me because you're trying to protect yourselves.*

I found that very hurtful after all we had done for her.

She said that she would have a terrible time in the Old City where she knew nobody. She said: *I'd be very lonely there. Here at least I've got you.*

I said she was sure to make friends very quickly. She looked unconvinced.

And then she demanded: *How would I manage without a ration-card?*

I had not thought about that. I said quickly that a different system was in force inside the protected area since numerous members of her community had entered it before rationing was introduced. (I had no idea if it was true.)

She just pursed her lips and shook her head in that maddening way she had. My wife lost control and grabbed her by the upper arms and said: *You have to go. For your sake as well as for ours. You're in danger here and you're putting us in danger.*

The girl said: *I won't go. And you can't make me. If you tie me up and carry me out, I'll kick and scream. And if you did get me as far as the Old City, I'd tell the police straightaway that you've been hiding me.*

My wife slapped her and screamed that she was a selfish wicked little vixen.

I pulled her off her and told the girl to go straight to bed and that there would be no supper for her.

Discussing it that night, we agreed the girl would get nothing to eat until she gave in.

* * *

My wife stayed in all the next day and made sure that rule was enforced. On the way home I explored some back-lanes and found a
dark corner nearby in which the girl and I could wait for the end of
the curfew. When I got home I joined my wife in her attempts to
persuade the girl that it was to her advantage to accept the plan. By
the end of the evening, however, she had not relented.

We agreed we would have to continue with that approach the
next day. Still, she would not give way. And so we had to carry on
with the harsh sanction for a third day.

That afternoon I went back to the Old City and found, as I had
feared, that the stream of people had dwindled to the point where
the officials were once again able to scrutinise the papers of those
entering.

As soon as I opened the door of the apartment, my wife greeted
me with a smile of relief and said: *She's backed down at last. I've given
her some lunch. She's agreed to leave tonight.*

I told her it was too late, and she almost wept with frustration.
I went into the living-room and found the girl sitting at the table
with an empty plate in front of her. She looked up at me and said:
*I've decided it will be better to go where nobody cares about me than to
stay where everyone hates me.*

I told her it was now too late. And I added that none of us
hated her.

I wasn't sure if it was true. There were times now when I found
myself feeling more anger towards her than I had felt for anyone.
And yet I knew that none of it was her fault. However, many of the
things she said stung me and lingered in my thoughts. The claim
that everyone hated her rankled, for example. We had bent over
backwards to make her welcome and accommodate her whims and
fads. There seemed to be no recognition in her of what her presence
was costing us in money, in hunger for my wife and myself, and in
danger for all four of us.

* * *

Until now at least there was the knowledge to sustain me that my wife and I had seen eye to eye on almost everything relating to the girl and that, apart from a few disagreements about how to deal with the situation, we had not argued. Unfortunately, this now began to change.

Perhaps because of the nervous exhaustion all these worries were causing me, I woke up the following Monday morning with a splitting headache and strong feelings of nausea. There was no question of my going to work.

My daughters went off to school and to work, and by twelve o'clock my wife had left for the orphanage. I was dozing and trying to read, and after about an hour there was a knock on the door and the girl came in. She was wearing a very short dress I had seen only once or twice and had put on lipstick.

With an expression of apparent solicitude she asked how I was feeling and if I needed anything. When I said I didn't, she sat on my bed and began to tell me how her father used to get dreadful migraines and what were the various cures he had tried and whether they had been effective. I said I didn't have a migraine but just a slight chill or something.

She said: *Are you sure? Where does it hurt?* She leaned forward and placed a cool hand on my brow. She said: *I think you might have a fever.*

She took her hand away and dropped it to my chest. While it rested there she drew her legs up on the bed in a sideways kneeling position. Her bare thighs were a few inches from my hands.

She said: *You don't mind me being here, do you?* She said it with such an expression of innocent concern that I had to tell her I did not mind at all.

She put her head on my chest and murmured: *I wish you were my daddy.*

After that I must have dozed off because the next thing I remember is the door opening suddenly and my wife saying in an angry voice: *I think you'd better go.*

It seems that both the girl and I had fallen asleep and lain there for a couple of hours until my wife got back from the orphanage and woke us up.

The girl jumped off the bed and ran out of the room.

My wife was quite irrationally upset. She told me that I had behaved extremely improperly in permitting the girl 'to sleep with me'. I protested that I had merely fallen asleep because of my ailing condition and had no idea she had been there. Probably because of the strain she had been under for so long, my wife refused to acquit me and said: *That skimpy little skirt! The makeup! You should have ordered her out of the room immediately. You must have realised what she was trying to do.*

We continued to argue, and to my astonishment my wife accused me of always having had an illegitimate interest in the girl from the very beginning. I was horrified and denied it. Had she really thought that? When had she started to believe it?

She brought up the private conversations I had had with the girl in my study when we were talking about a gift for my elder daughter, and then getting more worked up, she cited the period when I had been giving her lessons there.

Eventually I stopped defending the girl and conceded that she might have been trying to influence me, but I insisted that my conscience was clear: I had never thought of her as anything but a child like our younger daughter. My wife was clearly unconvinced.

I was off work for the next two days, and during that time my wife did not go to her orphanage. She said she wanted to stay at home and look after me, but I was afraid that was not her real motive.

Thinking about it afterwards, I began to recall how flirtatiously the girl had smiled at me and how knowingly she had allowed her short skirt to ride up her thighs when she drew her legs up on my bed. She was just fourteen, but she had a precocious grasp of how arousing that was for a man.

* * *

It was on my first day back that one of my colleagues told me someone had been looking for me. The stranger had been standing at
the other entrance to our building—the one I never used because
it was the longer way round—and asking people who went in and
out if they knew me. My colleague had replied that he had never
heard of me, for which I thanked him. In those difficult times, it
was always safest to reveal nothing. I asked him to describe the
man, and he said he was about forty, not well dressed, and from
his manner and speech, not well educated. I speculated about it for
some time. It was clearly neither the girl's father nor her brother.
My first thought was that it might be the man I was sure I had seen
in the Viennese cafe and again in the café opposite our apartment.
Yet that individual had been wearing a smart business-suit.

Could it be some messenger from the girl's family trying to
contact me? On reflection, that seemed highly unlikely. I could
see no way anyone could have connected the girl with my place of
work—unless I had at some point been recognised without realising it.

The most obvious means for the girl's family to find her was still
through the café, and so that afternoon I took the risk of going in
there and having a coffee and asking the proprietor if anyone had
been asking about 'the girl who used to come here with her family
on Friday afternoons'. He said not.

Then I passed the house once again and saw that the cards advertising the café were still there and were just about legible.

I continued to use my usual entrance to the building in which
I worked, but a few times I made a point of walking past the other
one on the opposite side of the street. I never saw anyone hanging
about near it. In fact, anyone doing that would have been shooed
away by the building's porters if he could not give a good account
of himself.

* * *

That week I overheard people at work complaining that the Old City was a hazard to public health because of the over-crowding and the breakdown of services like water and sewerage. I heard rumours about what was happening there: riots, acts of violence, the spread of sickness, and widespread starvation. At the end of the week, the authorities announced that it posed a threat to public health and would be closed down within a short period and its occupants 'processed for relocation'.

That Saturday evening my elder daughter arrived home late, and I happened to be in the kitchen when she came in for a glass of water. She sat down at the table with me and we talked. She told me that 'friends in the auxiliary police'—a distressing term!—had started work in the Old City. They were selecting people in certain categories—the old, the unwell, those who were mentally or physically handicapped—for relocation. I asked where they were being relocated, and she said vaguely 'somewhere in the East'. That was puzzling since our city was almost as far to the East as it was possible to go and still be inside the country. Beyond was the country that the Enemy had more recently invaded and conquered in the face of fierce opposition and which it was ruling in an even more brutal manner than ours.

I said: *The fact that they are sending the sick and elderly off first suggests that those who are able-bodied are going to be relocated to somewhere where they can maintain themselves by work.*

My daughter made no response, and I had the impression that she knew more than she was prepared to reveal.

This was the moment for a serious conversation with her about what concealing the girl was doing to her mother and sister. I told her I had decided that one way or another the girl had to go.

She said: *Of course. This apartment isn't big enough for five people. Not even for four. It would suit a couple with a child but that's all.*

I was surprised by that way of putting it. But I went to bed convinced I had to find a way to get the girl out of our lives by any means necessary, and that I had the full support of my elder daughter.

The next night as my wife and I were preparing for bed at about ten-thirty, we heard the sound of several cars screeching to a halt outside our building. We looked at each other in horror. Then we heard doors banging and shouts and people running up the stairs and realised it was happening in the building next door. After a few minutes the sounds started up again. We dared not look out of the window, but from down in the street we heard screams and blows and then car-doors slamming and the vehicles accelerating away.

Neither of us slept much that night.

* * *

When I got home the next evening I found my wife in a terrible state. It wasn't until the three girls had gone to bed that she was able to tell me why she was so upset. She had been told by one of our neighbours that the night before, a couple living in the next building had been arrested with their two children for the serious offence of hiding a young man who was a member of the girl's community.

She became more and more agitated as she talked about the danger to our daughters. She kept saying: *She has to go. You must get rid of her. She will be the ruin of all of us.*

I tried to point out that if we simply pushed her out she would be forced to wander the streets homeless and hungry. Inevitably, she would be arrested and then she would lead the authorities straight back to us.

She almost shouted: *You're making up excuses. You care more about that girl than our own children. You're going to kill us all for her sake. It's unnatural, perverse.* Then she physically attacked me, pummelling my chest with her fists until I grabbed her arms.

What most upset me was the absurd allegation that my interest in the girl was unnatural.

The only way I could calm her down was to promise to try to make contact with some underground organisation—of whose existence I had heard only the vaguest rumours—that helped people from her community to hide.

* * *

Everyone was afraid to talk about such matters, and so I knew it would be hard to find out what I wanted. I had already discovered how very difficult it was to approach any topic that implied unease with the current situation, even when I was with my closest friends. I realised it would be even more risky to attempt it with colleagues at work. Even if one of them appeared to go along with me, I could not be sure he was not trying to lead me into a trap. I selected one of my workmates who I thought might be trustworthy and began to hint at the issue. However, as soon as he realised what I was starting to imply, he changed the topic in the most abrupt manner.

Then I happened to overhear a man in another department saying quite loudly that some new regulation was 'inimical to our national interests'. I made a point of sitting beside him in the canteen the next day and, when we were alone, brought the conversation round to the political situation. We talked about it in guarded terms, but I had the impression he was prepared to be franker. Over the next few days I set out to win his confidence. Eventually, he began to talk fairly unguardedly about his hatred of the Enemy and his anger at the plight of our nation. After about a week I was becoming more and more confident about raising the question of getting help for the girl. But then to my dismay he said: *The one good thing they have done for us is to start getting rid of those damned leeches who've been sucking our country's blood for centuries.*

* * *

I don't know if it was because of the arrests next door, but from this moment my wife stopped going to the orphanage three afternoons a week, and so she was no longer getting a meal there. She was increasingly reluctant now to leave the apartment at all. She and the girl—cooped up together all day—squabbled and bickered ferociously.

The girl had become obsessed with the doll whose face had been smashed. She would sit in a corner holding it and repeating: *I still love you. I love you more than I ever did. We'll always be together. You and me and Mummy and Daddy.*

We all found that maddening—especially my elder daughter. She talked of the girl as evil, and said the doll was a talisman she was using to cast an evil spell on us. I didn't believe that, but I was worried her mere presence was endangering us.

Her consumption of a share of our food was threatening our health. As the rationing tightened, I saw its effects on the others. My younger daughter developed boils—perhaps because of some deficiency in her diet or a reaction to the foodstuffs we now had to eat: turnips, swedes, the fattest and most gristly parts of pigs and cows. I suspected my wife was starving herself to help her children and me. She became thinner and thinner. We had a set of scales in the bathroom, but one day it disappeared. I found it at the back of the cupboard on the landing and decided to leave it there. We were all losing weight, and I realised my wife was right that there was no point in measuring our loss.

The only one of us who was not driven mad by the girl's endless conversation with the doll was my younger daughter. She would often sit beside her and talk as the girl caressed the doll. I felt that the girl was exploiting my younger child's sweet nature by making her fond of her and therefore ensuring she would be her advocate when her own future was being discussed. And my daughter was paying a high price. One night she woke us with her screams, and when we rushed into her room we found she was waking from a nightmare. In tears, she told us she had dreamed that we—her mother and father—had become menacing and hostile towards her and had advanced on her with knives as if intending to attack her.

* * *

One evening about a week after I had gone back to work, there was a knock at the door. When I was sure the girl had run to her bedroom, I opened it. There was a stranger standing there. He was a burly man of about forty. He spoke my name and when I confirmed it, said: *Can I come in, sir?* His accent was that of an uneducated man brought up locally.

I said: *Might I ask what this is about?*

He said: *I'm a chauffeur, sir. At least, I am when I'm in employment.* Then he lowered his voice and mentioned the name of his last employer, and it was the girl's father. I stared at him, calculating rapidly. I was strongly tempted to shut the door in his face. But then I reflected that if he had found his way to me, he must know something, and if I slammed the door on him, he might go straight to the authorities.

I said: *I can't imagine what business you can have with me, but you'd better come in.*

I led him into my study and asked him to take a seat. Then, shutting the door behind me, I popped into the living-room and whispered to my wife to make sure the girl stayed in her room until our visitor had gone. I went back and asked him why he had come.

He embarked on a long rambling account which was often hard to follow. The gist was this: He had driven the parents of the girl and her little brother to what was then the capital. There they had been caught by the invasion and found themselves unable to return when that part of the country became the Western Zone. They were staying in the expensive hotel the girl had mentioned—he himself lodging in a cheap place nearby—and after a while the authorities came and invited the parents and their child to a reception-centre where they would be entertained at no expense. He said that with a sort of smirk, and I asked him what he thought a 'reception-centre' meant. He said with a look of wide-eyed innocence: *I have no idea, sir. I don't know why they were offered that accommodation or where they were taken.*

He said he got back to his employer's house only very recently, when he managed to get across what was now the national frontier between what had been the Western and Eastern Zones of our poor country, and he found that the house had been sealed by the authorities. There was nobody there since both the girl and the servant were missing.

His wife, who also worked for the family as a cleaner and occasional cook, told him that the servant at the house had mentioned to her (before she vanished with the things she had stolen) that the girl had gone to stay with the family of a man about whom she was able to tell him only what the servant had told her: his daughter attended the same school as the girl and they were close friends.

I answered that he had been misinformed and my daughter had hardly known the girl, and none of us had any idea what had happened to her after she had stopped coming to school.

He ignored that and maundered on about how he was worried about the girl and that was why he had come to ask me about her. He talked of his and his wife's affection for the child and his concern for her.

I was pretty sure that he was at the very least leaving out many things, and most probably simply lying.

I recalled my colleague telling me that a stranger had been asking for me at work, but I did not dare ask the man if it was he since I did not want to reveal where I worked, in case he did not already know it.

The chauffeur said he wondered if he should report to the authorities that the girl had gone missing.

I stared at him, and he boldly met my gaze. Did he really not know that the authorities were offering a large bounty for information about her whereabouts? Was this an elaborate way of hinting he would claim the reward by leading the police to this apartment unless I gave him money?

I made it clear to him that I still didn't understand why he had come to me.

He said he had gone to the school and enquired about friends of the girl who matched the description he had been given. Eventually he had learned the name of the family whose daughter had befriended the girl.

That sounded highly implausible because I could not imagine why anyone there would have revealed anything about a pupil to a man unable to justify his curiosity—and especially in relation to a child who had been withdrawn because of the new regulations.

If that was a lie, then how had he found me?

A thought came to me. Did he and his wife occupy an apartment above the coach-house? In that case, if he had been there on the night I explored the back of the house, had he been awakened by the noise I had made and followed me all the way home? I had believed that someone was dogging my footsteps. If so, I could see why he might not want to be truthful about how he had traced me. And that meant he was lying about having only recently got back from the former capital. And if it was he who followed me, why had he taken so long to come here? And had he followed me to my office? And assuming that was correct, why had he been hanging about outside my office asking about me?

Various possibilities occurred to me: Was the chauffeur in fact the husband of the servant who had stolen things from the house and disappeared? Instead of leaving the city, had she hidden somewhere in the locality? Their main aim would be to get into the safe, which someone had certainly attempted to do. Even if that were not correct—and the girl would be able to tell me if they were married—were they working together? Had she cheated him as well as her employers? But in that case, would she have told him anything at all about me?

He started talking about how hard things were in the present state of affairs for a man who was out of work and had a wife to support. I realised he was asking for money. If he was indeed blackmailing me, I was caught in the same paradox that had arisen with the concierge: if I gave him anything, it would confirm that I was frightened of him.

I told him I was very concerned to learn of his plight and that I myself was very hard-pressed financially or I would help him out with a small loan. I promised to keep my ears open for news of a post that might suit him, and I urged him to stay in touch. This seemed to me to be a good way to keep open the possibility in his mind that I might give him cash and deter him from reporting what he knew to the authorities. And it signalled that I had nothing to be afraid of. Yet if he knew of the reward, surely nothing would stop him going to the authorities?

I could see how disappointed he was that I was not offering him money. When I stood up, he remained seated.

He started talking about the girl and saying that she must be somewhere. Then he said: *You know her family belong to that community? How* could he think I did not know? I just nodded. He said: *They're looking for anyone like that and sending them into the Old City. There's all sorts of stories going around about what's happening there. What I think is that some family she is friendly with might be hiding her because they don't want to let her be sent there.*

I said: *I suppose that's possible.*

He said: *What worries me is that they might be caught. It only needs a tip-off to the right people and they'll send the Special Police round. I've heard of several cases. They search the apartment and if they find someone hiding who should be in the Old City, they arrest the whole family. Everyone, sir, including the kiddies. They take them away and nobody knows what happens to them.*

Was he threatening me? If he was, then his acting talents were impressive. His voice cracked with emotion as he spoke.

I agreed that it was very sad, and eventually he realised I was not going to change my mind and got up and left.

When he had gone, I called my wife into the study and recounted what had just happened.

She was horrified that someone had learned of our link to the girl's father. As for the news that the family had gone to a 'reception-centre', she found that reassuring and said: *So they might come back before long?*

I said: *I don't think we should be encouraged by that. I don't know what 'reception-centre' means. I think it might be a form of detention.*

She asked: *What shall we tell the girl?*

I said: *Simply the bare facts as we know them.*

She went to fetch her and then left us alone. I told the girl that her father's former chauffeur had just come to see me. She didn't seem to find that surprising. I asked her what she could tell me about him?

First she demanded to hear if the man had told me anything about her relatives.

I answered: *He told me that your family were invited to a reception-centre some months ago.*

She cried out and clapped her hands: *Oh what wonderful news. I was wondering where they had gone since I know they don't have friends near the old capital.*

She skipped around the room for a few moments. Then a thought struck her and she said: *But why haven't they sent a message? Why haven't they come back?*

I shrugged. *The border between the two zones is still hard to cross.*

She asked: *What's a reception-centre?*

I told her I didn't know. She was indignant that I had not pressed him on the subject.

At last she answered my question about the chauffeur and told me that he and his wife—who was not the servant who had made off with the valuables—were nasty sly people, and her father had recently been on the point of dismissing both of them. They did, as I had guessed, live above the coach-house at the end of the garden.

Thinking about the interview afterwards, it occurred to me that it was the chauffeur who had telephoned the girl's house from the former capital after her parents and younger brother had been taken away. Had he said to the servant that this was their opportunity—he, his wife, and she—to steal things from the house? Did the servant then cheat him by purloining valuables before he returned? Did the chauffeur know about the safe? If so, did he return earlier than he was now pretending and try to open it? Had he subsequently succeeded? Would he have the nerve to do that and then stay on in the coach-house? Or would he dare to come to me? Why would he bother if he had taken what was in the safe? What had been in the safe? Was it still there?

* * *

That afternoon I once again walked to the Old City, but this time I found I was not allowed anywhere near it. I circled it and found that the area of exclusion now embraced the cattle-market just outside the Old City, where trains running towards the conquered territories in the East stopped to offload or pick up livestock for slaughter.

* * *

When I got back I found my wife and the girl shouting at each other. The girl was now proclaiming her intention of going to the reception-centre the chauffeur had mentioned and rejoining her family.

When I entered the room, she turned to me and said: *Daddy owes you so much money. Let me go and ask him for it.*

I said: *You can't get across the frontier without the right papers. They'll arrest you. You wouldn't even get out of the city.*

She said: *You don't want me to go, do you? You're just scared I'll put the police onto you. But think how much money Daddy will give you when I tell him about you.* Before I could stop her, she picked up the pocket-book with the schedule in which I had been entering expenses incurred by her and studied it.

I tried to snatch it from her, but she sprang away and turned the pages. Then she looked up at me accusingly and said: *You've stopped keeping a record. You stopped weeks ago. Why did you do that?*

I said: *No reason. I just realised that in these uncertain times your father might not have much money by now.*

She glared at me: *Why do you say that? That's not true. I'm going to go to them. Daddy's rich. He can look after me.*

I said: *You're safe here. If you go out there you'll be picked up.*

She said: *I'm going and you can't stop me.*

With those words she flounced out of the room. I hurried to the front-door and locked it and put the key in my pocket. How ironic that only a few weeks ago I was desperately trying to make her leave and now I was determined to stop her.

From now on the door had to be kept locked, and my wife and I had the only keys. This meant that one of us had always to be there to let our daughters in and out. And we could only leave the apartment together if we locked it behind us with the girl inside, which we were unwilling to do.

* * *

That evening, when all was quiet, I discussed with my wife the implications of some of the things the chauffeur had said. She agreed with me that it was hard to tell how much he knew and whether he was trying to extort money by making a veiled threat. The remarks he had made about 'tip-offs' and 'visits from the Special Police' were particularly alarming, we both felt. I pointed out that if he did report his suspicions, there might be a search of the apartment at any moment. The girl could not stay where she was. It was too dangerous for her and for all of us. And yet we could not think where she could go.

And then one of us thought of the attic.

* * *

Because ours was the top-floor apartment, we had a trap-door into the roof-space above the building. That made the attic a reasonably secure hiding-place as long as the searchers had not been told of its existence, and fortunately the trap-door was in the tiny dark utility-room and therefore not easily noticeable. However, as my wife pointed out, if a really thorough search of the apartment were made, the attic would surely be examined. And it seemed virtually certain that anyone searching the apartment would have been told about the attic by the concierge or a neighbour.

The next day I made the trap-door even harder to spot by rendering it flush with the ceiling and painting it and the whole ceiling black.

The girl would have to be up there all the time because if the police came to the house, there would not be time to get her up a ladder, shut the trap-door, and move the ladder to another room. The longer we took to answer the door, the more suspicious they would become, and the greater the likelihood they would investigate the trap-door.

That would not protect us, of course, if it were the concierge or her son who reported us since they would have told the police about the roof-space. However, if the police searched the apartment after being tipped off by the chauffeur, there was at least a chance they would not know about it.

Late as it was, we began to make preparations immediately.

There was no floor up there but merely joists. We dared not think of buying boards since carrying them past the concierge would arouse suspicion. For the present we would have to use a makeshift. I brought the step-ladder to stand under the trap-door and opened it and measured the gap. I had to move carefully to avoid making a noise that would bother our neighbours below. Then I unscrewed the door from a small wardrobe in our bedroom and, with my wife's help, just managed to get it through the trap-door and lay it across the joists. That would have to serve for now as both a bed and a daytime seat. My wife hung a curtain where the wardrobe's door was missing, so its absence would not be noticeable.

It was now about two in the morning. My wife went to rouse the girl, and a few minutes later I heard a scream of fear and anger. The girl was distraught at being told what she had to do.

She had a horror of spiders and rats and of the darkness. She guessed that the attic space was dirty, cobwebby, and dark. My wife explained that she would have to lie doubled up on the wardrobe door with only folded-over blankets as a mattress. Now my younger daughter was crying as well at the prospect. The girls' mutual resentments were forgotten. The noise wakened my elder daughter, who came out in her nightgown and was equally appalled at our decision. I kept having to shush all of them. If we made too much noise it would be talked about in the building. My wife and I were now paying the penalty for having shielded the three girls from the knowledge of just how dangerous our situation was.

In a whisper we told them how things stood. The chauffeur might well have gone straight to the police, and in that case they might arrive before dawn. I promised that the girl would only have to stay up there for two or three days. If the search had not been carried out by then, we could assume the man had not reported us.

The truth was that my wife and I had agreed it was not safe for the girl to be in the apartment now. She would have to stay up there day and night from now on.

The girl at last consented. I went up the step-ladder carrying a torch and then balanced myself on the joists as the girl, still in tears, awkwardly climbed up after me. I handed her the torch and told her to use it as little as possible. It was bitterly cold up there. I hated what we were having to do. I climbed down, shut the door, and put the ladder in the kitchen.

My wife and I hardly slept that night, listening to the girl's sobs from above us and dreading the sound of cars drawing up outside or heavy steps on the stair. We felt that the girl was crying at least partly as a bid for our sympathy. We would have to make her keep quiet for fear that the neighbours in the adjacent apartment on the top floor might hear her. At the point where I was about to go and move the ladder back and open the trap-door and tell her that, she stopped weeping. She must have cried herself to sleep.

There was no raid that morning. I left for work having moved the ladder into position and opened the trap-door. The ladder was too heavy for my wife to move quickly on her own. I told her the girl must stay up there the whole time apart from calls of nature. Each time she returned, she must close the trap-door after her. If my wife heard anything that sounded like a search-party approaching, before opening the front-door, she must drag the step-ladder into the corridor if she was unable to take it any further.

* * *

When I got back that evening my wife had nothing ominous to report. However, the girl was in a very distressed state. She had spent almost the entire day in the dark, alone, unable to read one of her beloved magazines, and barred even from listening to the wireless.

We dared not let her have a light or a wireless because the cables would have to trail back into the apartment, and a wireless might be heard in the neighbouring building or by someone coming to our door. And at night a light might be seen through loose slates—especially since the blackout was being enforced by wardens.

That evening I organised what I called 'emergency drill' in which we practised what to do if we guessed there was about to be a visit from the authorities. Each of us had different tasks, depending on who was in the apartment at the time: my wife alone, my wife and younger daughter, my wife and myself, and so on. It was important that each knew his or her specific task in each set of circumstances: who would ensure the trap-door was closed, who would move the ladder, and who would open the front-door once the signal was given.

Later my wife and I talked about what I should say and do if the chauffeur came back. We decided that if he revealed he had any piece of evidence which would be solid enough to justify his going to the authorities, I should give him money—ostensibly to tide him over while he looked for work. But what we would do after that, heaven alone knew.

We decided that I would keep in the apartment a large sum of money in cash—a month's salary—to bribe him or in case of any other emergency.

Over the next few days I set about raising that money, and I found I could do so only by borrowing at an extortionate rate of interest. I had no choice but to accept those terms.

* * *

At the office the next day I heard people talking in hushed voices about rumours they had heard concerning what was happening in the Old City. It was being said that large numbers of people were being marched to the cattle-market and put on trains for 'relocation'. Nobody seemed to know what that meant.

All day and most of the night, we had to hear the girl weeping and snivelling, and although it was hardly her fault, it was getting on our nerves. Once my wife snapped and screamed through the trap-door: *Why can't you just go away! Stop existing! Why did you ever come into our lives?*

That wasn't the only noise we heard at night. Now we were often wakened in the early hours by previously unheard trains that went very slowly towards the East and stopped for long periods while the engines continued to rumble and let off steam.

* * *

That night I waited up until my elder daughter came in. She was very obviously the worse for drink. I asked her to sit down and tell me what she had heard from her new friends in the auxiliary police about what was going on.

She started telling me how they joked about what they were doing in the Old City, but as she spoke, it was clear to me that she was horrified by it. I asked her to explain 'relocation', and she told me. I understood at last how naïve I had been. I thought back to my concern that the girl's beautiful house should be safeguarded for its owners, that her family's store should be properly run, and to my absurd schedule of accounts for an eventual reckoning with her father. And I realised that the reason why the authorities could not interrogate the girl's father about his assets was because he and his wife and younger son had been 'relocated' very soon after the capital had fallen to the Enemy.

I told my daughter not to breathe the slightest hint of what she had told me to my wife or the two girls.

On the rare occasions when I spoke to the girl after this, I found myself resenting her for her conviction that she would soon be restored to her relatives and for the fact that she needed to be lied to.

* * *

I encountered her only briefly and rarely, however. All the rest of the next day and the next she stayed in the attic. Food was passed up to her just twice a day, and she was allowed to descend for a call of nature just twice. Whenever she did so, she badgered my wife or me, if I was at home, to allow her to stay down in the apartment. We had to tell her to be patient.

After she had spent three nights and two days up there, we were obliged to inform her that we were not allowing her to descend to the apartment until further notice. She went berserk and screamed that she was going to spend her whole life up there. The Occupation was never going to end. She would die up there. We were trying to kill her.

We had no choice. It seemed that the chauffeur had not reported us—but at any moment he might decide to. And there were other dangers: the concierge and my brother-in-law. Not to mention the mysterious stranger who might or might not be taking an interest in us. And our former domestic.

And yet we knew this could not go on indefinitely. Rationing and price-rises were reducing even further what my wife and I had to share with the girl to the point where we were both tired and listless most of the time and suffered from boils and mouth-ulcers. The girl needed very little since she was lying prone all day doing nothing, but at the same time, she was an adolescent and was growing.

Every night now, my wife and I would lie in bed talking very softly because we knew the girl was above us and just a few feet

away. As the days had passed, she had grown increasingly disturbed and we had become more and more concerned about her
behaviour.

* * *

We had other worries. My elder daughter was still keeping late
hours with the concierge's son. Then, on the evening of the fifth
night the girl had spent in the attic, I had further reason to be
alarmed about my daughter. She came running up the stairs very
late and burst into the apartment in tears. I saw her in the hall, but
she dashed into her room and would not open to my knocking or
even her mother's calls. I suspected that the concierge's son had offended her, and I could guess how. I talked it over with my wife. She
pointed out that we dared not have an open breach with the young
thug and his mother since we were in such a vulnerable position. It
was a delicate situation.

We managed to get our daughter alone the next morning, and
she more or less confirmed that my surmise had been correct. She
said the man had been hinting he knew the girl was still in the
apartment, and he had said it as if to put pressure on her to comply
with what he wanted. I told her to try to hold him at bay without
actually offending him. She gave me and her mother a look that I
will never forget.

Our younger daughter was causing us concern in other ways.
She was now waking almost every night with screaming nightmares. And even during the day, whenever she heard a step on the
stair she started as if she had been struck.

* * *

The girl had been hidden above our heads for two weeks when the
concierge's son stopped me as I was leaving for work and told me
he needed to get into the attic. I asked why, and with an insolent
smile he said he needed to do a routine check on the roof before the

weather deteriorated. That was transparently spurious. Determined to show no alarm, I said he had never done a 'routine check' before, and I had occupied the apartment for many years. He grinned rudely and said that was all the more reason to do one now.

Then he asked in a meaningful manner if I had any objection?

I said I had none at all, but he would have to come at a time arranged in advance to suit my family's convenience. We settled on the following evening at six. I told him he should bring a step-ladder since I did not have one.

As soon as I got home that evening I told my family we would have to hide the girl in the bathroom during the lout's so-called inspection and we would have to conceal all traces of her presence in the attic.

We rose very early the next morning, and my wife and I got the girl down. I lowered into the apartment the wardrobe-door and everything else she had used, and tried to restore that part of the attic to its original state of filth. Then I hid the step-ladder in a cupboard in the kitchen. We would have to risk keeping the girl in the apartment all that day.

I managed to leave work a little early and was home by a quarter to six. The plan was that the girl would remain in the bathroom during the 'inspection', where my younger daughter would be noisily running a bath and splashing about. My elder daughter sulkily agreed to hang around and talk to the concierge's son in order to distract his attention if that was needed.

He arrived a little before six, and it went almost to plan. When he saw the trap-door he said: *You've made it flush with the ceiling and painted over it. Why is that?*

I said: *My wife thought it would look nicer.*

He made a show of clambering up the ladder he had brought and then clumping about overhead. When he came down, he said: *There are signs of leaks up there. Have you had any water-penetration down here?* I assured him we had not. He asked if he could go round looking and, having anticipated that he might find some pretext for this, I readily agreed. We went solemnly from room to room, and nothing betrayed the presence of a third girl. My elder daughter was reading a magazine in the sitting-room and they began to chat. I left them and talked to my wife in the kitchen.

After a few minutes the young man left the sitting-room, and he and I resumed the search of the house. When we got to the bath-room he asked if he could wait until it was free. I said my younger daughter was often in there for hours. He said: *She wouldn't mind wrapping a towel around herself and letting us in for a moment, would she? After all, she's just a kid.*

I didn't like that. I thought there was quite a nasty tone in his voice and a look in his eye that worried me.

I managed a chuckle as I said: *She'd better not have heard you say that! But you're very welcome to come back in an hour or so.*

He shook his head ungraciously and, to our relief, left.

As soon as he'd gone, we reversed everything: we put back the ladder and the wardrobe door, and the girl returned to the attic.

* * *

Ironically, the conversation our daughter had with the concierge's son while he was in the apartment seemed to have had the effect of healing the breach in their relationship. For the following evening she was out with him again and returned as before, very late and fairly tipsy. I talked to her about it the next morning, and she said: *I can't have what I want and he and his friends are amusing enough and have plenty of money to splash around. I might as well throw myself away on them since there is nothing else available.*

* * *

That afternoon when I reached our building I was struck by the sight of a man standing on the opposite side of the street gazing up at it. He looked to me like an official out of uniform, and I even wondered if he was the stranger I believed I had seen watching me weeks ago.

* * *

About ten days after we had begun to conceal the girl in the attic, my wife and I agreed that our elder daughter had become quite surly and ungracious towards us. We challenged her about it, and she said she resented the fact that despite our 'snobbish contempt for the concierge's son', we were prepared to get her to 'lead him on' in order to protect ourselves and the girl.

We tried to persuade her that we were not in any sense asking her to do anything shameful but merely to keep him from avenging himself against her by doing something that would cause serious harm to all of us. She said he would soon turn nasty if he didn't 'get what he was after'. The bluntness of her language upset both of us.

After that she virtually stopped speaking to us except when it was absolutely necessary. But she also gave up going out in the evenings. She would sit reading while the three of us chatted or listened to the news on the wireless and talked about it. Or she would spend the whole evening alone in her room.

* * *

I was no more immune from the effects of what we were doing than the others. Now I jumped at my own shadow on the wall of the close. I started in the street if I thought I heard my name called. I found myself staring at strangers as they approached along the pavement, terrified they would accost me with some new horror. But I knew it was taking an even heavier toll on my wife, and I saw worrying signs of a return of the problems she had had three years earlier. I was sleeping badly, but I knew she was suffering worse insomnia because whenever I woke during the night, I found her already awake.

* * *

Just a few days later, what my wife and I had dreaded seemed to take place. That night our daughter went out and did not come back to the apartment. By midnight we were in despair. I hardly slept and was woken by her trying to sneak in quietly at six-thirty. My wife and I decided to say nothing about it to her.

* * *

It was the next day that the air-raid siren went off. There had been practices once a week at six on Sunday evenings for several months, but this was nine o'clock on a Wednesday evening. It was clearly for real and not a test, though we hoped it was a false-alarm. I had worked out what our procedure would be, and everyone did what they were supposed to do. My wife and I had agreed that if there was an air-raid, we would have to let the girl come down. She would be in a state of terror alone up there, and the attic was the most exposed part of the house if a bomb should explode nearby. So I ran to get the ladder, and I raced up it and opened the trap-door and told the girl to come down.

Then the three of us joined the other two crouched under the table in the living-room. The siren had changed from the sound meaning 'attack imminent' to the terrifying shriek which meant 'attack in progress', and after a minute or two our worst fears were realised when we heard a muffled crumping sound like a huge pancake being dropped. There was another and another and they were becoming more frequent and getting louder and louder.

I honestly believed I was going to die in the next few minutes. Now we could feel a slight juddering a moment after each explosion. We were all in tears by now—myself included—hugging each other and telling each other how much we loved each other. My wife and both daughters embraced the girl who was laughing and crying in the strangest way and babbling that we were her family and she loved us all. I heard my wife telling her how sorry, how

desperately sorry she was, for what we had had to make her go
through, and I joined in, telling her we loved her as much as our
own daughters and we had banished her to her dark hiding-place
because it was the only way to save her life. She didn't seem to know
what we were talking about and just kept saying: *From now on I'll be
with you always, Mummy. Kiss me, Daddy. You're never going to leave
me again, are you.* She was clutching the nearly shapeless object that
had once been the oriental doll and kissing it and repeating: *We'll
always be together. I'll never let you leave me again.* I kissed her and I
kissed the girls and my wife. Everything we had argued about in the
last months seemed utterly trivial.

My younger daughter was telling the girl she didn't mind about
the made-up stories and she didn't hate her for telling lies or having
lovely dresses and expensive dolls.

The bangs reached a terrible climax when there was one that
was so loud it hurt our ears and the building shook so that our
knees bounced on the floor and I was sure the whole thing was
going to collapse. But it didn't. The bomb had fallen a hundred
metres away, we found out later. It had brought down one of the
neighbouring apartment-buildings and killed fifteen people. When
the thuds had faded into the distance and the siren had switched
to the 'all clear', we crawled out from under the table and were
astonished, I think, to find that everything was the same. Outside
we could hear alarms going off and bells ringing and people shouting as the emergency services dealt with the direct hit. But inside
the apartment there was a calmness like the sea after a storm. (Of
course that first bombing-raid was just a mild foretaste of what was
to come, though we had no idea of that at the time.)

It was heart-breaking to have to tell the girl to go back up. She
stared at us uncomprehendingly. The raid seemed to have destroyed
her reason, and she appeared not to understand where she was or
who we were. We led her to the trap-door, and then she started
screaming and trying to get away. We all had to hold onto her, but
she fought back, kicking and biting but somehow still clasping the
doll. I had to grip her from behind, pinning her arms so she was in

pain if she tried to move. I shouted to my wife to get a towel and then told her to wrap it round the girl's head so it would go into her mouth, letting her breathe through her nose. We managed to do that, and it was horrible, but it was the only way to stop her screaming.

It was already too late. Someone knocked on the door, and I sent my elder daughter with instructions to use the chain to see who it was but to let nobody in under any circumstances. She came back to say that it was the nasty old man from the joiner's family, and he was complaining about the noise and asking who was making it. I told her to say that her younger sister had become hysterical because of the bombing and then to shut the door immediately.

Something occurred to me later: *Why would someone be bothered by screams when there had been loud explosions and when there was still uproar outside? Did the old man suspect something?*

By now the girl was exhausted from her struggling and screaming. She went limp and was in a sort of trance of exhaustion. With great difficulty we three adults managed to get her through the trap-door and lay her on the wardrobe door.

An hour later the girl must have come round because she started screaming and hammering on the trap-door which, luckily, she could not open from that side.

After just a few minutes I had to go up the ladder and stop her. The noise was being heard at least on the floor below and probably in the neighbouring top flats. I had no alternative. I had to grab her and then lie on top of her holding her arms with my weight and with one hand, and using the other to gag her. After god alone knew how long, but it might have been the best part of an hour, she stopped thrashing about and again fell into a sort of sleep.

I came down and talked alone with my wife. We agreed we would have to start putting ground-up sleeping-pills in her food to keep her sedated. And I would try to make a sort of strait-jacket out of an old sleeping-bag our elder daughter had used when she went camping.

* * *

We could not risk another such episode for fear that the police would be summoned by our neighbours. And I was terrified of such a fit of hysteria happening while I was out of the apartment because my wife was not big and strong enough to do what I had had to do.

Because of our fear that we had aroused the suspicions of neighbours, over and above the concierge and her son, a new and even stricter regime now had to be introduced. We had to put a chamber-pot up in the attic and have her hand it down when we passed up food. And that was now done just once a day instead of twice.

One consequence of all of this was that we had to keep our younger daughter at home in order to maintain the pretence that it was she who was creating the noise.

My wife and I made a decision: we would stop talking about the girl in the presence of our daughters unless it was unavoidable. It was a problem that we and not they had created, and as far as possible we should shoulder the burden alone. Both our children had already made sacrifices for the girl and were continuing to do so.

Therefore, when my kind-hearted younger daughter asked that morning if she could sit in the utility room under the trap-door and talk to the girl and do things she could share like listen to the wireless, we refused permission saying that it was too risky since a neighbour might hear. This was true, but the real reason was we wanted her to forget, as far as was possible, that the girl existed.

After the bout of hysteria, the girl was calm for the rest of that day and the next. We assumed that was the effect of the sleeping-pills my wife had ground up and put in her food. After only one more day, however, she complained that there was a nasty taste in the food and stopped eating it.

When she had consumed nothing for two days except water, my wife and I discussed what to do. We agreed to stop putting the drugs into the food and take the risk of her becoming violent again. However, she still refused to eat and muttered sullenly that we were trying to poison her.

At the end of the third day, my wife said she would keep on offering her food once a day, and if she chose not to eat it, that was, after all, her decision.

There were times when we sat together as a family listening to a concert on the wireless and were able to forget about the girl, even though I was aware she was lying a couple of metres above us in the darkness.

On the fourth evening the wireless announced that the cleansing of the Old City had been completed, and it was now being fumigated before being opened to allow members of the national population to move in.

It had become clear to me that one or other of the people who knew about the girl was going to go to the authorities—if they were not already alerted. My family was facing disaster.

It was about now that my elder daughter talked to me in private and said: *Mother can't take any more of this. You've got to do something. The family has to come first.*

* * *

On the fifth day after the girl had virtually stopped eating, there was a knock at the door while we were having supper. When I opened it, using the chain, I saw it was the chauffeur, and he was grinning. I led him straight into my study and closed the door. He started a rambling account of his unsuccessful attempts to find employment. I hardly paid him any attention since I was trying to work out what I should do and was also listening in case the girl realised we had a visitor and started—god help us!—calling out to be rescued or something like that.

Then I became aware that the chauffeur had brought the topic round to a conversation he had recently had with a neighbour 'just round the corner' from where he and his wife were living in the coach-house. This woman knew various things about the girl's family, he said. I realised with horror that he was talking about the friendly maid-servant in the house next door to the girl's.

The man rambled on, and it emerged that this woman had told him the authorities wanted to find the girl and they had offered a reward. He named the sum, and as he did so he looked at me with a speculative gaze. He explained it was so large because the authorities were convinced the girl was in possession of various bonds and bank-notes that she had removed from the house when she went into hiding.

I said: *This is all very interesting. I'm not sure why you think it concerns me, however.*

With an insolent smile he answered: *Well, that's the thing, you see, sir. This woman told me something that struck me as very significant. One day a few months back a gentleman came to the house next door and asked a lot of questions about the family that had lived there. He had been there a few weeks earlier. She told him all about the servant who had made off with lots of valuables from the house and he seemed very inquisitive considering he said he was just passing by. While they were talking she noticed a taxi about thirty metres along the road. At one point she looked at it and saw a girl getting out who looked very like the missing kid. She quickly got back in again as if she knew she wasn't supposed to be seen. The man went off and the woman watched out of the window and though he went off in one direction, a few minutes later he came back from the other direction and got into the taxi and it drove off. Isn't that a curious story, sir?*

After that it was clear he was threatening me. However, I kept up the fiction that I wanted to help him out with a loan. I went and found the cash I had been collecting in a drawer in our bedroom and gave all of it to him. It was about half the bounty being offered for the girl. I knew he would keep coming back for more and more, and when he had extorted from me a sum several times larger than the reward and I had no more to give him, he would report me to the authorities and claim the bounty.

When he had gone, I went back to the study. I sat there for some time and went over and over what had happened and how I had got into this position. At one point my wife tried to come in, but I asked her to give me more time. I told myself that if I had not helped the girl for the past few months, she would be dead by now. My family and I had made huge sacrifices and taken enormous risks for her and had received in return nothing but spite, ingratitude, and threats. It was she who had brought this on herself. She had disobeyed my instructions by getting out of the taxi and by doing that, she had made it inevitable that the link between her and myself would become known.

I called my wife into the study. She asked if I had had to give the chauffeur money, and I said that I had. I told her the man had shown me that I had to find a permanent resolution to the issue, and I was going ahead with it. Our anxieties would be over very soon. When she asked what I meant, I told her to trust me and to ask no questions.

* * *

That night I encouraged the rest of the family to go to bed at ten. Then I went into the kitchen and ground up about twenty sleeping-pills and put the powder inside a small piece of meat and rolled it up and secured it with strips of bacon. (It was the family's entire meat ration for the week.)

There was an interval of about an hour between the time the concierge usually closed her hatch—about ten o'clock—and the eleven o'clock curfew, and since it was now winter, it would be dark.

I left the apartment shortly after ten-fifteen. I took off my wristwatch and put it in my pocket.

I walked around until I found one of the stray dogs that had become more and more of a nuisance as the War had gone on. It swallowed the meat in one gulp. I stayed with it and followed it around as its pace slowed and fifteen minutes later it stumbled and collapsed on the ground whimpering. I took off my coat and picked up the animal and, hiding it in my arms, I hurried towards the canal. I stopped to pick up a loose brick. There was a road-bridge over the canal not far from my apartment, and under it, where it was very dark, there were steps down from the towpath. I descended them and knelt on the lowest step and, dropping the coat on the ground, thrust the unconscious dog under the freezing water. By some reflex it began to struggle. I had anticipated that and holding its body with my left hand, brought the brick down as hard as I could on its head. It stopped moving and I held it under the surface for several minutes. Then I let go, and the corpse sank slowly out of sight into the oily black water.

When I got home I washed and went into our bedroom. My wife was in bed but awake. As I undressed I said to her: *Don't even speak to me, please.*

* * *

In the morning while my daughters were making ready to depart, I took my wife aside and told her to put the strongest drug possible into the girl's food if she took any sustenance.

All that day at work I went over and over what I had to do that night.

I hardly ate a mouthful at supper that evening. We were all very subdued. It was as if the others knew that we were close to a terminal point.

My wife told me the girl had refused everything except water. Just before ten I told my daughters to go to their rooms and stay there until the morning. They made no protest. Then I asked my wife to do the same, and she obeyed without even speaking.

I went up the ladder and opened the trap-door. I told the girl I was going to take her to someone who would smuggle her out of the city and take her to her parents.

There was silence, and then at last she answered in a low un-steady voice and seemed to be saying she would come with me. She was so weak that I had to climb up and virtually carry her down the ladder. She was clutching the doll.

I led her into the hall and wrapped her in a spare overcoat be-longing to my younger child. When I opened the front-door she said she wanted to say goodbye to my wife and daughters and to

thank them for all they had done for her. I told her they were already asleep and it was very late.

When we had almost reached the ground floor, I told her in a
whisper that I was going to carry her past the concierge's hatch for
safety. I picked her up and she was as light as a child half her age. I
hurried past the hatch, which I could see was closed.

I heard something fall and realised she had dropped the doll as
I picked her up. I didn't put her down. As I carried her I was weeping so that it was hard to find my way along the rubble-strewn path
towards the bridge. She was so light. Just before getting home that
evening, I had left a brick on the steps under the bridge. Mercifully,
I didn't have to use it.

When I got back I found the doll lying on the floor near the
concierge's hatch. I took it up to the apartment and went into the
kitchen, and taking a knife, I cut it into small and unrecognisable
pieces and put it into the bin for the household waste. I did that
because my younger daughter would know the girl would not have
abandoned it voluntarily.

I went into our bedroom. My wife was waiting for me, and I
crawled into the bed fully clothed and put my head against her
shoulder and lay like that for several minutes. Neither of us spoke.
She just put her hand on the back of my head and pressed me to
her.

Eventually I was able to speak. I told her the girl had gone, and
we must now hide any sign that she had once been concealed in
the attic. So, late as it was, we both got up and started work. I took
down the wardrobe door once more, and while I fastened it back
where it had come from, my wife searched around and under the
joists with the torch until she was sure there was no trace of the
girl's presence there. I put the ladder back in its usual place.

It was after two when we got back into bed. I had expected to
feel an enormous sense of relief—as well as other, terrible emotions.
I felt nothing. The impact of what I had done did not hit me until
several days later, and that was partly, I suppose, because of what
happened immediately after I had got into bed that night.

I was only dozing fitfully when, a couple of hours later, I heard a rush of feet up the steps and a loud hammering at the door. There was nothing to hide now, and I opened it as quickly as I could. There were three members of the auxiliary police and an officer in charge, who was from the Special Police. He looked very like the stranger who seemed to have been following me and whom I thought I had spotted in the café and then in the bar and elsewhere, but because he was wearing a uniform I could not tell if it was he.

The officer was perfectly courteous but offered no explanation of who or what they were looking for or why they had come. His men were carrying a step-ladder and first went to the trap-door and searched the attic space. Then they made a thorough examination of every other room.

I was told to wake up everyone in the apartment and assemble them in the living-room. My sleepy younger daughter emerged looking bemused, but when she saw the uniformed men she started in fright. I signalled to her with what I hoped was a reassuring smile that all was well. She, like her sister, must have thought the girl was still in the attic.

The search was lengthy and thorough. Nothing was found, of course. The officer supervised the men very closely while the four of us sat in silence in the living-room waiting for them to finish. The officer did not speak to anyone but myself and certainly said nothing to my elder daughter. Finally, he thanked me for my co-operation and apologised for having disturbed me and 'my delightful family'.

When they had gone I told my daughters that the previous night I had taken the girl to some of her own people who would help her to get to safety. Neither of them looked at me as I said that.

The fact that the men had gone straight to the trap-door showed that the search was not a random one. It was clear that someone had betrayed us. It could not have been the chauffeur, I was sure, because it was in his interests to milk me for as long as he could. And he would not have known about the hiding-place in the attic.

The more I thought about it, the less probable it seemed that the officer was the man who had appeared to be following me. He was too high-ranking to have done that. And if a stranger had started to spy on me, that simply shifted the mystery to the question: who had tipped him off? I could not stop thinking about the way in which our former domestic had suddenly turned up on the flimsiest pretext. She knew the girl belonged to the alien community, and she had reason to have a grudge against us for having dismissed her. On the other hand, she had never displayed any sign of resentment about that and had always seemed genuinely fond of the two younger girls.

Was it the old man in the joiner's family? Had he guessed the girl's origins months ago while she was making frequent visits to his apartment? Had he made an offensive remark to her and was that why she had fled his apartment in tears that day? And had he then, months later, heard her screaming and realised that we were hiding her?

Or had my brother-in-law betrayed me in the desperate hope of somehow rescuing his wife and children? Or was it my former colleague?

The concierge and her son were the most obvious suspects. Realising that I was not going to bribe her to keep quiet, she might have opted to turn me in—perhaps not even knowing of the specific bounty on the girl's head. And heaven knew what mixture of spite and vanity might have prompted her son. When I talked to the woman in the next few days, I had the impression that she was somewhat chastened. I was sure she felt no guilt towards me, but she might have received a frightening rebuke from the Special Police for sending them on a fruitless mission.

The timing was extraordinary. A few hours earlier, and the searchers would have found what they were looking for.

I am aware that some time later—when the events I've recounted became known—people said various things about who had reported the girl's presence in the apartment, and some of the allegations were cruel and preposterous.

My assumption about the chauffeur was confirmed when he came back just two weeks later. I told him I could not help him any further, and when he began to bluster and threaten, I told him I had been the victim of unfounded allegations that I had hidden someone sought by the authorities. I described the raid by the Special Police and told him he was more than welcome to go to them and ask them to carry out another search. He looked horrified and left quietly.

A few days later I was alone with my elder daughter. We had not mentioned the girl since the day of the raid. Now I talked briefly of what we had been through since we took her into our apartment all those months ago. She listened warily without speaking. I talked of the various issues we had faced and raised the incident of the smashed doll. I said I didn't believe our domestic had done it. My daughter said nothing.

* * *

I still have nightmares about those few minutes when I carried the girl in my arms that night, and over and over again I wake up shaking with horror and believing that it is my own little daughter I am holding.

* * *

By the time the fighting around the city and the air-raids had intensified about a year later, I was so deeply in debt because of the loan I had raised to pay off the chauffeur that I had no means of sending my wife and children to safety. A few of my colleagues had influence with the authorities, and enough money left after the steep inflation we had suffered, to be able pay for their families to move to the countryside. My indebtedness and my difficulties at work deprived me of that option.

When the War ended, I was still grieving the death of my wife and younger daughter in one of the final bombing-raids. They died in a nearby shelter when it took a direct hit while I was at work in my office. Ironically the apartment-building was undamaged.

My surviving daughter was at work, having found a position in a department store. She is employed there still. She shares an apartment near it with two other girls, and since it is on the other side of the city, I don't see her very often.

When the concierge and her son denounced me to the Liberation Authority for murder, I had no inclination, at first, to offer any defence. Only in the last few weeks have I found the desire to write this account. My motive has not been to avoid the death penalty, for I have nothing left to live for. My intention has been simply to offer a record of what I went through. Others can make a judgement of my conduct as well as I can.

Acknowledgements

I owe a huge debt of gratitude to my fellow-novelist, Liz Jensen, for her insight and her encouragement.

About the Author

CHARLES PALLISER is an American and an Irish citizen who has lived most of his life in the United Kingdom. He read English at Oxford and after gaining a postgraduate degree, taught at the University of Strathclyde in Glasgow. In 1990 he became a full-time writer when his first novel, *The Quincunx*, was an international best-seller. It was awarded the Sue Kaufman Prize for First Fiction by the American Academy and Institute of Arts and Letters and has been translated into a dozen languages and sold more than a million copies in English. He has subsequently published four more novels: *The Sensationist, Betrayals, The Unburied,* and *Rustication*. He has taught English Literature and Creative Writing at several London universities, at Rutgers University in New Jersey, and at the University of Poitiers in France. He was the first Deputy Editor of *The Literary Review* when it was founded in 1978. He has had one stage play produced and the BBC has broadcast two radio plays and a short film for television.